AUGUST 1944:
THE ANCIENT CITY OF STRASBOURG

Outside the sprawling, block-long Maison Rouge Hotel all was strangely quiet. Squadrons of SS police had cordoned off the surrounding square and stood guard at the lobby entrance to keep out all without passes.

The focal point of attention that day was the third floor. It held nearly a hundred German industrialists and military men. Their agenda was starkly simple: the planning for survival after defeat.

Thirty years later, that plan is about to bear its bitter fruit . . .

The
Strasbourg Legacy

William Craig

A BERKLEY MEDALLION BOOK
published by
BERKLEY PUBLISHING CORPORATION

For Eddie, Jimmy and Anne,

**WHO HAVE ALWAYS BEEN
SUCH GOOD FRIENDS.**

Library of Congress Catalog Card Number: 75-12795

SBN 425-03263-9

*BERKLEY MEDALLION BOOKS are published by
Berkley Publishing Corporation
200 Madison Avenue
New York, N. Y. 10016*

BERKLEY MEDALLION BOOK ® TM 757,375

Printed in the United States of America

Berkley Medallion Edition, NOVEMBER, 1976

The Strasbourg Legacy

1

Adolf Hitler's voice on the radio was unmistakable. Shrill, forceful, it assured the people of Germany that the Fuhrer was alive and well. It also promised swift vengeance on those who that day had tried to kill him. Within the borders of the Third Reich, Nazi justice was already being dispensed.

In a Berlin courtyard Count Klaus von Stauffenberg lay dead under the focused headlights of several trucks. They illuminated his bullet-torn uniform and the Iron Cross he had won for valor.

A short distance away, General Ludwig Beck, who was supposed to head the new government, slumped in a hallway. The bullet he had fired into his brain had failed to kill him. One revolver shot into his neck by a guard had been the coup de grace.

Instead of assuming command of the armed forces, General Erwin von Witzleben was at home, saying farewell to his family. The bewildered officer had no escape route planned but knew he had to flee. The secret police would find him within hours.

In Paris, General von Stuelpnagel released SS officers and men he had imprisoned and fled to the countryside. Near Metz he placed a gun at his temple and shot himself. The bullet only blinded him and he was taken prisoner by his pursuers.

The men who plotted to destroy Adolf Hitler and the Nazi regime had committed the one unpardonable offense. They had failed to cut off the head that ruled the body. And now they would pay the supreme penalty: death, but not quickly in most cases. In the cellars of the Plotzensee and Prinz Albrechtstrasse, torturers were beginning to pry secrets, names, dates from victims unable to withstand the torment. It would be only a matter of days before thousands of conspirators would be dragged to extinction.

At Army Group HQ in Russia, General Henning von Tresckow was resigned to death. For more than a year he had been a traitor to the Nazi regime and when he received a private call telling him the plot had failed, Tresckow laughed bitterly, for he knew firsthand how difficult it was to kill the Fuhrer. Only months before he had secreted a brandy bottle on Hitler's plane. Inside the bottle was a bomb scheduled to detonate high over the Ukraine. But the timing mechanism failed and Hitler landed safely, totally unaware of the attempt to kill him. One of Tresckow's friends retrieved the evidence and destroyed it, leaving the general free to continue his vendetta. But when Stauffenberg's bomb failed to kill the dictator, Tresckow had no illusions. He would be found out in the roundup of enemies of the state.

After writing a last letter to his family, he walked off into a nearby meadow. When he reached a deserted spot Tresckow pulled out a grenade, held it to his head, and died in the violent explosion that followed.

General Tresckow had escaped the only way he could from the police state that would have broken him. He knew the power of the Schutzstaffel, the black-uniformed SS, and he chose not to fall into their hands. And in this moment of crisis for the embattled Reich, legions of SS men were performing their assigned tasks with the ardor they had shown ever since Hitler chose this group as his elite corps of bodyguards, both for him and for the nation. Always loyal, never questioning edicts from the leader, the SS had waged a war of extermination across Europe. They ran the gas chambers, the concentration camps, the mass shooting galleries, the experimental farms where human guinea pigs ostensibly furthered the cause of science. And now it was an easy chore for them to track down the wretches who had attempted assassination and a coup d'etat.

By the second week in August, barely three weeks after the bomb blast in Rastenburg, the secret police had pleased Hitler immensely. By that time, they had given him a list of the major plotters, and had captured almost all. Hitler praised their efficiency and urged them on to even more sadistic heights as they broke bodies to gain more information. In the SS, at least, Hitler realized he had a force that would protect him to the end.

That end seemed near. And all the time Heinrich Himmler's men were carrying out Fuhrer decrees unhesitatingly, SS leaders vigorously prepared for a life of their own, if and when Germany collapsed. Adolf Hitler was never to know this. His deputy, Martin Bormann, did know and he managed to cloak the efforts in secrecy. Bormann had given the ultimate order to his Brotherhood of Comrades, for he too planned to carry on with or without the Fuhrer. The canny peasant from Bavaria had no intention of perishing in a final Götterdämmerung.

In early August 1944, Allied armies in France had already broken out of the Normandy beachhead and begun the drive for Paris. Southwest of the French capital, General George Patton's Third Army was across the Sarthe river and rushing toward the bridges of the upper Seine. Not content with merely trapping the battered Wehrmacht in France, Dwight Eisenhower was urging his armored columns to strike for the German border itself and make it impossible for the enemy to dig into a defensible line.

One hundred and twenty-five miles east of Paris, the ancient city of Strasbourg lay directly in the path of American tankers. Swollen with thousands of German troops looking for lost units, it was a bedlam of traffic jams and angry voices. But outside the sprawling, block-long Maison Rouge Hotel all was strangely quiet. Squadrons of SS police had cordoned off the surrounding square and stood guard at the lobby entrance to keep out all without passes. The lobby was almost deserted. A few high-ranking officers wandered the carpeted halls. Waiters, all soldiers, paid them scant attention as they hustled to and from the kitchens.

The focal point of attention that day was the third floor. Requisitioned weeks before by the SS, it now held nearly a hundred German industrialists and military men, who had arrived for twenty-four hours of intensive conferences. Their agenda was starkly simple: the planning for survival after defeat.

In Conference Room A more than fifty men sat around a gleaming mahogany table while the speaker, a short, red-faced officer, resplendent in his black SS uniform, read from a memorandum:

"Lufthansa flights to Spain have brought out more than three hundred million deutschemarks in American dollars and British pounds. Of the pounds more than half are counterfeit but so perfectly done that no problems are anticipated in marketing them.

"As to the report on bogus corporations, at this moment more than six hundred have been established, a third in the Middle East, some in Spain, but most in Argentina, Chile, and Paraguay. I cannot give you precise information on their locations since such lists could fall into the wrong

4

hands. A master list has been made, three copies have been secreted and in time will be utilized. Any questions?"

A civilian, scowling under bushy eyebrows, stood up.

"My company would like more explicit news on distribution of its assets. We don't want to disperse any more funds without it."

The SS officer stared coldly at the questioner. "You're a corporation lawyer, aren't you?"

When the man nodded, he went on abruptly: "Let's straighten this out right now for everyone in the room. All money funneled through the economic section of the Schutzstaffel will find its way into overseas development. None of it will stick to the fingers of any man in the organization. We didn't come to Strasbourg to rob you. We came to set up a future for all of us after the Third Reich ends. We're all in this together." The SS man glared around the table. "Any more questions?"

There were none and the meeting droned on with a discussion of the establishment of research institutes to produce new weapons for the time period 1950 to 1960.

In Conference Room C, down the hall, a less formal atmosphere prevailed. Only five men had gathered here, around a table heaped with food and drink. Two were from the Reichsbank, Hitler's national repository for loot from conquered countries. The other three men held high office in the SS; the senior of this group, a tall, extremely thin man, whose hooked nose dominated his pinched, lean face, was talking rapidly, gesturing with his right hand in a broad sweep. "I tell you the front's been ripped apart. The only reason the Americans haven't broken deep into Germany is because they ran out of gas. That damn Patton is better than Rommel." He shook his head in frustration and picked up a piece of ham, which he chewed energetically. "What's the latest on the Max Heiliger account?" he suddenly asked. He was referring to a special SS account in the Reichsbank.

One of the bank officials clapped his hands in glee. "I don't know what to do with Max anymore. He's so fat he's about to explode." Everyone laughed until the hook-nosed man shook his head. "That could be bad with time running out on us. Aren't the pawnshops doing their job?"

"The pawnshops are begging off now. They have too much to sell and not enough buyers from the general public."

"Damn it, they're getting a chance at the best jewelry in the world from those Jews in jail. And what about all the gold from the Auschwitz teeth?"

The banker was almost apologetic. "Too much. You're sending us more than we can handle. The vaults are filled to the ceilings."

The hook-nosed man nodded to an aide. "Take this up with the appropriate section. Tell them to melt the gold down faster and ship to Swiss banks, you know the places. . . . Spread the wealth so we can get our hands on it later. Otherwise, Patton himself will capture it."

While his assistant solemnly wrote down the instructions, the hook-nosed man went back to the table and piled a plate full of potato salad. As he took his first mouthful, the crump of exploding bombs drifted through the windows from the west. The hook-nosed man ignored the intrusion and went on with his meal.

Many SS leaders knew they faced war crimes charges. Convinced also that defeat would lead to chaotic conditions within Germany, these Nazis felt they could remain unnoticed inside the enemy camp while the Allies hunted down the most famous criminals, like Goering, Ribbentrop, and the rest of the hierarchy. Then in the apathy born of victory and sated emotions, hard-core SS men could make a more leisurely departure from occupied territories.

Thus ODESSA—Organisation der SS Angehörigen (Organization of SS Members), a secret underground escape group—came into being. On maps of the world, men sketched projected routes to freedom. They all led south, through Austria to Italy, through France to Spain, and then on to South America or the Middle East. Individual way stations were not marked as yet. These safe places would come later, as SS experts refined details. In the meantime, they were content to lay out broad outlines and disburse monies necessary to make the underground work successfully. The Maison Rouge conference was merely a beginning.

Nine months later the war was over, the victors swarming over a prostrate Germany. And what the SS planners at Strasbourg had predicted, happened. The roads, villages, and cities of the country became clogged with human refuse, the uprooted, dispossessed, and faceless. Into this dispirited mob went the most notorious men of the dead Fuhrer's regime, the thousands who had run his police state and killed millions of innocent victims.

Heinrich Himmler put on an eye-patch and posed as a farmer. Seized at a roadblock by British troops, he finally admitted his identity and asked to see Eisenhower. His interrogators thought he might divulge SS secrets if they treated him well and in fact Himmler hinted several times that he could tell much about Bormann and others. But the sudden appearance of another British officer changed all that. The new arrival ordered Himmler stripped and searched, and in panic the SS leader bit into a cyanide capsule concealed in a tooth cavity and fell to the floor in agony. Despite the use of stomach pumps and emetics, Himmler died in fourteen minutes.

Rudolf Hoess, the commandant at Auschwitz, was as unlucky. Discovered working as a farmhand near Bremen, he freely confessed his role at the most infamous camp in the history of the world. Fully cooperative with his captors, Hoess balked only once. When asked to sign a typed confession, he remained adamant until one offending passage was changed. Hoess refused to take credit for killing three million inmates. He had been on leave of absence while a portion of them died in the shower rooms.

But the list of captives was pitifully small. More than fifteen thousand men who had played vital roles in the extermination of so many simply vanished: Franz Stangl, commandant at Treblinka; Josef Mengele, doctor at Auschwitz; the Maurer brothers, mass killers in Russia; Adolf Eichmann, charged by Hitler with responsibility for the final solution of the Jewish problem; and Martin Bormann, heir to the throne, supposedly seen on a Berlin street, dead from artillery fire, later, "seen" near the Danish border heading for a waiting boat, a wraith wrapped in shadows.

And then, as postwar problems took precedence, the Allied powers tired of the chase. The Nuremberg Trials disposed of the most visible Nazis, and the hangman's noose choked the breath from a few of the men who had murdered millions. Meanwhile, mutual distrusts between Russia and the West intervened, and statesmen now juggled nuclear weapons in treaty discussions.

In the submerged world of the SS, men began to stir and the highways to safety became visible to those seeking safe passage. The money so carefully allotted years before provided a guarantee of immunity. More than seven hundred and fifty overseas companies were now funneling funds back into the escape networks. In the towering Alpine resort area close to the Austrian border, secreted millions were dug from the ground, pulled up from lakes, withdrawn from friendly banks. Men who had waited two years, four years, for the signal stealthily moved south, always under the direct protection of bodyguards, former SS soldiers, who themselves had functioned so anonymously in the camps that hardly anyone lived who could identify them as guards once manning machine guns or dropping Zyklon B tablets into gas chambers.

Adolf Eichmann went out through Austria, into Italy, where a monastery provided sanctuary until he boarded a ship bound for Argentina. Franz Stangl used the same route of escape. So did Mengele, Johannes Richter. So, too, did Martin Bormann and hundreds of others.

Behind them, in Germany itself, these leaders left a cadre, thousands of Kamerads who had sworn the oath of allegiance to the Brotherhood of the SS for life and would obey any summons calling them back to service. In the interim, they had been told to gradually resume normal lives within the new nation of West Germany.

2

On the night of March 11, 1945, a German submarine, the
U-155, broke the surface of Tokyo Bay and turned east-
ward toward a rocky coastline. A mile offshore, crewmen
launched a boat and headed into a beach. They had no
trouble finding the landfall, for the sky was a flaming,
smoking red from the previous day's bombing of Tokyo
by American B-29s, which had left the Japanese capital in
ruins and more than 100,000 people dead in the rubble.

In ten minutes, the German sailors touched the shore
and immediately dragged three heavy boxes inland for a
quarter of a mile. Beside a deserted cottage, under a
forlorn mimosa tree, they dug three deep holes, buried
their cargo, and slipped back to the waiting boat. Behind
them two men lingered for a moment. One was Haupt-
mann Erich Lottman, an SS officer. The other, Colonel
Kantaro Onishi, commanded a garrison of secret police in
the Tokyo district. Six years before they had been friends
in Berlin, when Onishi was an observer at Gestapo training schools. Now they hurriedly scribbled on pieces of
paper, which they exchanged and countersigned. Lottman
saluted briskly and offered his hand in farewell. Onishi
took it and bowed low in friendship. Then Lottman was
gone and within a half hour the U-155 had dived for the
deep waters of the Pacific.

With the war ended and Japan soon competing for
world economic markets, Kantaro Onishi prospered.
Always a man who cultivated the important people, he

swiftly rose in the business world. By 1972, he was recognized as an industrial genius, president of an enormous electronics firm and a director of banks, museums, other corporations.

Onishi commanded homage from all, for his new career was built on integrity and impeccable ethics. Each year, on his birthday, he received thousands of good wishes from employees and friends, honored both to know him and work for him. Always included in these congratulations were greeting cards from Herr Erich Lottman. Mailed from different parts of the world, they gently reminded him of the old days and mentioned a long overdue reunion at his country home.

Onishi knew the cards were from strangers, for just after the war he had made inquiries through American friends and learned that Lottman died in prison awaiting trial for crimes committed in Poland. So for more than a quarter century, the Japanese businessman waited patiently, and during that time he faithfully visited his country house on the eastern shore of Tokyo Bay to make sure no one had disturbed his secret. The grass grew wild around the mimosa; silent and rundown, the cottage remained empty all those years while Onishi marked time.

On November 9, 1972, as the industrialist was being driven home from work, his car telephone rang and he heard a voice say: "May I be the first to wish you well on your birthday?"

Onishi chuckled: "But it's not for two months yet. Who is this?"

"Erich Lottman."

Onishi's hand tightened on the receiver.

"The reunion is tomorrow. The bank that Fuchida runs. Your friend from the secret police, remember?" The voice was sarcastic and Onishi was annoyed.

11

"All right, all right. Twelve o'clock in the vault."

The caller hung up abruptly and Onishi sat quietly, staring blankly at the streams of traffic outside his window. Stirring himself, he ordered the chauffeur to change course and head for the eastern shore of Tokyo Bay.

He worked all night, digging up the iron chests left by Captain Lottman so long ago. For a sixty-year-old man it was exhausting, but he dared not entrust the work to anyone else, not even the chauffeur, whom he sent back to the city. Before dawn Onishi had tugged the boxes out of the ground and then collapsed on a mat in the cottage for a brief sleep. At eight A.M. he walked a mile to a village and called his office, canceling all appointments for the day. At nine he phoned his close friend, Fuchida, the bank president, and told him to meet him with a panel truck. Two hours later the executives were in the vault, staring at more than five hundred gleaming bricks, emblazoned with the Nazi swastika.

"Don't ask me, Masao. Just figure out its worth and transfer it when I tell you."

"But that's at least twenty million dollars' worth there."

"Just add it up right. I want nothing to go wrong for either you or me."

"What are you afraid of?"

"I'm not sure . . ."

The door opened and a tall man, stiffly erect, entered quickly. Without a word he handed Onishi a scrap of paper, faded by the years. It was Lottman's receipt for the gold, signed by Colonel Kantaro Onishi on March 11, 1945.

He kept looking down at it, not doubting its authenticity, just shocked at seeing it again.

"Is that adequate proof?"

12

Onishi brought his gaze back to the stranger, who had a noticeable crescent-shaped scar over his left eye.

"It is, yes of course. That's all I needed."

"Good. This other paper has instructions for delivery of the money overseas. I expect the exchange within thirty days."

Fuchida glanced at the orders and nodded.

"Thirty days is fine."

"Then it's settled."

"Of course."

The man turned abruptly and disappeared from the vault.

Onishi slumped into a chair and rubbed his chin slowly. Then he reached for the receipt from twenty-eight years before, lit a match, and touched it to a frayed end of the paper. As he watched, Erich Lottman's signature and his own blackened and vanished into ash.

On January 11, 1973, a messenger arrived in a Zurich bank, presented identification, and was led to a numbered deposit box. Fifteen minutes later he left carrying more than three million dollars in a black Gucci briefcase. Within a matter of hours, he had landed in Munich, where the first portion of Kantaro Onishi's treasure began to circulate.

3

Doctor Wilhelm Alt was well pleased with himself. The American couple answering his ad had just agreed to rent the upstairs apartment for double what any German family would pay for accommodations in Kronberg. At the front door he shook hands with the husband and waved farewell as the couple walked down the narrow steps to the street. When they drove away toward Wiesbaden he noticed another car moving quickly into the vacated parking place. A man wearing a dark topcoat got out and looked intently up at him.

"Herr Doctor Alt?"

"Ja." Alt instinctively started down to meet him. "Can I help you?"

The figure had moved under a streetlight and waited until the doctor came close.

"I'm sure you can. Josef asked me to talk with you."

"Josef, Josef who?"

The man thrust a photograph at him and Alt adjusted his gold-rimmed bifocals to look. The picture was of a uniformed man, perhaps thirty-five, and he was smiling. Alt knew that smile immediately because of the triangular gap between the front teeth. "Mengele," he groaned, and his visitor took him gently by the arm and helped him into the front seat of the car. Alt was trembling while the man went around and got in on the driver's side.

"Relax, doctor, I just came to give you a job."

"A job?" Alt's voice was lifeless.

"Tomorrow you fly to Berlin to identify a recently discovered skeleton. You are to confirm it is Reichsleiter Bormann."

Alt's mouth opened in amazement, but the other man's voice was now harsh, commanding.

"It's all arranged. Your reputation as a pathologist will help seal the verdict."

"Is that all you want?"

"Is that all?" The stranger roared with laughter. "My friend, at the moment, it's everything."

He handed the doctor an envelope and reached across to open the door. "A little something for your troubles, too."

Alt stumbled onto the sidewalk and watched dazedly as the car eased away from the curb and went around a corner. Mounting the front steps slowly, he wandered on into his study and sat down at the desk. Across from him the wall clock chimed nine times and he absently followed the moving pendulum. Back and forth, back and forth, just like Mengele's riding crop at that siding in Auschwitz; right to the labor barracks and a little more life, left to the gas chambers and ovens of Birkenau.

Alt suddenly noticed his reflection in the glass front of the clock case. He had always prided himself on his still-dark brown hair, but it distressed him to see how it was receding in front and thinning badly on top. The harsh lines around his eyes and on his cheeks only confirmed his depressing diagnosis. I'm shriveling up from age, he thought as he poured some cognac and sipped it sadly.

Again the pendulum caught his eye . . . left, right . . . Mengele . . . Auschwitz . . . left, right . . . twenty-eight years and yet they had found him, had waited until he would be useful again. Even though he had changed his name at the end of the war, had made a totally different life for himself, they had been watching him all the time, and then they pounced. Pounced as they had in the old days, on the pitiable refugees that fell out of cattle cars and formed shapeless lines on the railroad platform. Mengele was almost always there, examining Jews from all over Europe, even checking their teeth as though they were horses, before flicking the crop one way or the other. And Wilhelm Alt, then Heinz Linge, had been there beside him, making notes when Mengele found interesting specimens for future analysis. For Josef Mengele was not just a doctor in charge of disposal; he fancied himself a scientist and used Auschwitz as an experimental station for his passion, the study of twins.

Alt refilled his glass with cognac. Like those eight-year-old Hungarian boys, one crying because he had scraped his knee and it was bleeding, Alt had taken out a handkerchief and cleaned the wound while the boy stopped sniffling and looked gratefully up at him. And then Mengele had called for the twins and Alt followed them into the immaculate offices, where they disappeared into the testing area, holding hands. Two weeks later, Mengele handed Alt some papers and he typed a fifteen-page report on Mengele's findings about two Hungarian Jews, aged eight, who had been dissected after fatal injections of cyanide. Alt cried that day, and that night he borrowed a horse and rode wildly across the fields. But he was back at his desk in the morning and never once thought of asking for a transfer. At times the stench from the crematoria made him drink himself to sleep. Frequently he found excuses to avoid roll calls at the siding.

When the Russians came, Alt ran away with the refugees, and he had forged a new life for more than a quarter century. But now it was over, for they had found him, again, had evidently always known where he was.

The clock chimed ten, and Alt rose unsteadily, and went into the bathroom. Pouring a glass of water, he stared into the mirror at his pale, sagging face and thought sadly that he really should have gotten a toupee. Then picking up a bottle of sleeping pills, he went on into the bedroom and sat in a chair by the fireplace.

Incredible how they had traced him. And now all his career was worthless, because he would have to compromise his integrity again for those people. Alt looked around the comfortable room, at the framed photos, affectionately inscribed—photos taken over the years with young men from his hiking club. With a sigh, he turned away and his gaze settled on the envelope the SS man had given him. The doctor got up, retrieved it from the table, and tore it open. He was holding a neatly banded packet of American bills, ten thousand dollars in all.

Alt sat down and counted the money slowly. He stacked it in twenties, fifties, and hundreds, then swooped it all into a pile in front of him. At least his new companions were generous men. And might be again, it occurred to him, if they needed his special services. He put the sleeping pills back in the bathroom cabinet and began to pack for the trip to Berlin.

Ever since he had returned from a Russian POW camp in 1955, Horst Clemens had followed a precise daily schedule. Each morning at seven, in his garden apartment in Bad Homburg, he wrapped a wine-colored silk robe around his still-lean body and made himself a breakfast of croissants and black coffee. By eight-thirty he had trimmed his graying Van Dyke beard. At nine, armed with a carved walking stick, he started hiking through the heavily forested city park, and promptly at twelve emerged near the waterfall by the old castle. At twelve-thirty he was settled into his favorite chair at the corner table of the dining room in the Hotel Dreesen, where he ate alone. Except for Tuesdays, that is, those magnificent hours when he and four other former members of the Wehrmacht used the same corner table as a strategy board, where they laid out maps and refought battles from Thermopylae to Normandy. Horst was always the recognized leader in these seminars, though heated arguments raged around some of his conclusions. His credentials were impeccable when it came to military affairs. One of the most decorated combat engineers in the German army, he was a legend for his battlefield exploits. On this Tuesday, Clemens had prepared well; for more than an hour he dissected for his comrades the tactics employed by both armies at the Marne in 1914. While he lamented von Kluck's stupidity in moving the German right wing east of Paris instead of sweeping west of the city, he could not help but praise the flexibility of the French army under Joffre, which had confounded the rigid German order of battle. "Flexibility, gentlemen, is something the Wehrmacht needed badly when things went sour from 1942 on, particularly in Russia."

Then it was three P.M., which always came too quickly on Tuesdays for Horst Clemens. His friends rolled up the maps, drained their schnapps, and said goodbye until next week. And he was left alone with the empty glasses, his notes on war, and his still-fresh memories of the old days when he was needed and respected.

A bellboy came over. "Herr Clemens, a message for you." The note said: "Oberst Ullrich will call at six P.M."

Clemens left the Dreesen in an ebullient mood. It was eight years since the battalion reunion when he had last

18

talked to his commanding officer from the war. He worshipped Ullrich, the man who had taught him the engineering skills that made him so famous in the army. Ullrich, Die Mensch, fearless under fire, a friend who talked him out of taking his own life after his mother and five sisters had been killed in a bombing raid.

Clemens plunged back into his daily routine, entering the forest by the castle and walking briskly now toward home and the contact with Ullrich.

At five-thirty, he entered his second-floor apartment, opened up a bottle of Beck beer, and went over to sit by the phone. A yellow envelope lay propped against it. It had not been sealed or postmarked, just placed there by someone during his absence.

Clemens took out a passbook and an airline ticket. The passbook, made out to him, listed a balance of fifty thousand deutschemarks, deposited that day in the Dresdner Bank. The airline ticket was for a round-trip flight to Cairo. The return date was open; departure time was eight-thirty A.M. on April 30, 1973, two weeks away. As Clemens tapped the passbook against the table in consternation, the phone rang and he looked at his watch: six P.M.

"Oberst Ullrich?"

Clemens heard the voice of his mentor asking whether he had opened his mail.

"Yes, sir, I have, but I don't understand."

Ullrich began a detailed explanation.

4

The private screening was being held in a rundown building in the Soho district of London. The screening room itself, however, was elegantly furnished; oriental rugs, Monets and Picassos on the walls. Four men sat in expensive, brown leather chairs. The viewers were all in their fifties, well dressed, neatly manicured.

A microphone crackled and a voice filled the room. "Shalom, gentlemen. I'm sorry to bring you here on such short notice but we have something unusual this time."

A shaft of light illuminated the screen, there was the click of a slide projector, and a blurred figure appeared. Suddenly the image snapped into focus, revealing a man standing in front of an office building. Another slide filled the screen with his face, squinting through the sunlight at some unseen target.

"Tokyo, November of last year," the moderator explained. "He stayed at the Okura Hotel for three days. During that time he took one sightseeing trip to the eastern shore of the bay, bought two Nikon cameras on the Ginza, and spent one evening with a girl at a nightclub in Roppongi. On his last day in Japan he stopped at the Nippon Bank for ten minutes, then went out to Haneda and flew Lufthansa bound for Rome. But at Beirut he shook our man and disappeared."

"Are we supposed to know him?" a man asked from the row of chairs.

"Take a look at the crescent scar just above the left eyebrow."

"It's Richter! He's on the loose."

"Exactly, Malcolm. Our Johannes Richter from Paraguay, the butcher of Cracow. When he moved from that apartment building in Asunción, we followed him all the way to Tokyo. Now as to why he went there we still don't know, but beyond that we have to wonder what the hell brought him out of his safe hole in the first place."

Another slide moved into place and the audience stared at a group of Nazi officers, smiling stonily into a camera.

"The man to Heydrich's left, the tall one. And now the closeup." The officer was thin-faced, gaunt almost. His nose was hooked, the mouth pursed. His eyes seemed lifeless, blank.

"The mystery man. August Bleemer. Age then thirty-four. Education Göttingen, Heidelberg. Joined the SS in nineteen thirty-six. Soon one of Heydrich's pets, he directed the program to eliminate mental defectives within the Third Reich. Bleemer rounded up the retarded, the sickly, and sent them to quack doctors all over Germany and Austria. At euthanasia he was the expert. Our records show he was responsible for killing more than three hundred thousand people, not just Jews, mind you."

"But we've never found a trace of him, Hersch."

"That's correct. In nineteen forty-five, Bleemer submerged. While most of his friends left by way of Italy, he may have gone through Spain. A contact thought he saw him hanging around a dock in Cadiz but had no way to make sure. That was in nineteen forty-nine.

"We spent a lot of time looking for him after that. But though we were able to flush someone like Eichmann we had only a shadow in Bleemer. He had a wife in Stuttgart,

21

but she remarried and he never approached her. A daughter moved to Africa and died in the Congo uprising in nineteen sixty. A rumor, nothing more, that he showed up in Cairo for talks with Nasser in nineteen sixty-one. That's all . . . but what do you make of this?''

The next slide showed a man sitting on a stage next to a speaker's rostrum. ''The village of Markgröningen, a recreation hall there on the night of May fourth this year. The occasion a rally for the conservative wing in opposition to Brandt. Normal so far, but the man before you is a surprise. Karl Radel, age sixty-four, behind-the-scenes lawyer for various corporations, mainly in contract negotiations with labor. Has several homes, Essen, Dortmund, and a chalet in Lindau on the Austrian border. Up until this moment his politics seemed middle-of-the-road, nothing extreme; he has contributed to many candidates, he has close ties even to Brandt's group. Lately, however, and this really is one indication, he has been appearing at fund raisings and the like. When he speaks publicly, he stresses two themes . . . law and order and fear of Communism. He comes out strongly against a deal with Moscow.''

''What's he heading for from this?''

''No one knows yet. Maybe a plunge into politics in a big way. In the meantime . . .''

Another slide was up and it showed Radel talking from the rostrum. The picture had been taken from the side of the stage and showed him in profile.

''Anything strike you?''

In the silence the projector clicked on another shot, the original closeup of August Bleemer blended with the latest of Karl Radel.

''The nose, the damned hooked nose. Look at those two pictures.''

22

"There can't be two noses like that anywhere," said someone from the darkened room. "But why didn't he have plastic surgery?"

"Probably because he thought no one had a picture of him. His SS files disappeared, with all photos. He always stayed in the background, like Bormann, and who knows, he may be vain enough to like it the way it is."

"That picture of him with Heydrich?"

"That's the one he forgot. It was taken by Heydrich's own cameraman and later that day he was driving back to the lab when some underground fighters blew him up with a grenade. With the car in little pieces, Bleemer must have assumed the film was destroyed but it was picked up by a friend and eventually delivered into our hands."

"How did he get back into Germany? Didn't you say he went out by way of Spain?"

"He must have gone to South America for awhile but then returned in the fifties. Radel's dossier shows he spent four years in the Wehrmacht, two on occupation duty in France and two on the Russian front with the Two Hundred and Ninety-fifth Infantry Division. Wounded once, Iron Cross First Class, invalided home in nineteen forty-four, worked as a laborer until cleared by the Allies, then practiced law again. Clean bill of health as we would expect."

"Well, what do we do? Kill him?"

"You know better than that. After the mess over Eichmann, the Knesset will never approve it. We can't even make him have an accident until we have the proof about him. For the time being let's just watch Radel. Maybe he can lead us to bigger fish."

The lights went on in the screening room and the eighty-fourth meeting of the group had ended. Acting under direction of the Shin Bet, the Israeli intelligence service,

23

these five men pursued a lonely assignment. Though retired officially from active duty, they continued to hunt the people who had been the architects of the "final solution." But for the five men leaving the rundown building in Soho, it was a source of deep satisfaction, for each of them had a common bond. As sonderkommandos, working under the guns of SS guards, they had pulled members of their own families out of the "shower rooms" at Auschwitz.

5

The summer sun beat mercilessly on the CIA headquarters complex in Langley, Virginia. During lunch hour, many employees took their sandwiches and drinks into woods dotting the vast acreage and found some relief from the humidity. Lying in the grass or propped against trees, they ate their food and talked of such mundane matters as higher interest rates, skyrocketing prices, and pennant races in the major leagues.

At the same time, inside the administration buildings of the intelligence center, other employees sat in glassed-in cubicles and discussed such diverse items as covert operations in progress, defectors needing asylum, and the future impact on the agency of the ongoing Watergate hearings across the river in Washington.

At Langley, it was just a normal day in the abnormal world of global espionage.

JUNE 30, 1973
TEL AVIV TO LANGLEY—
SHIN BET WONDERS WHAT WE HAVE ON POSSIBLE NEO-NAZI INFLUENCE IN CURRENT ISRAELI-ARAB CRISIS. HEAVY SHIPMENTS SMALL ARMS ARRIVING ALEXANDRIA FROM NON-REGULAR SOURCES. THREE VISITS TO CAIRO THIS MONTH BY KNOWN WORLD WAR II CRIMINALS. ADVISE.

Matthew Corcoran chewed the earpiece on the frame of

his glasses as he weighed Archie Lawton's words. Corcoran, at forty-seven the most knowledgeable American on Russian subversion techniques, had for the past year been posted to Langley as a teacher, drawing upon his own experiences to advise trainees about to go operational.

The enforced deskwork showed its strain on Corcoran. Normally chunky for his medium height, he was now developing a paunch, his ruddy cheeks were puffy. His shock of red hair was perpetually mussed from running his hands through it in frustration. In his unpressed clothes, he looked particularly rumpled next to the neatly tailored men and women working with him. He ignored his appearance. His co-workers, in turn, made no comment about the sunglasses he wore most of the time to hide his bloodshot blue eyes, or the peppermints he chewed constantly.

The work, quite simply, infuriated Corcoran, who drank heavily in Georgetown bars and stayed away from home for days at a time. His wife Tessa had seen it happen before. Whenever Matt felt stymied by the system, he rebelled in the same way, punishing himself and those closest to him with bourbon. It was one way he chose to escape the tedium of headquarters. Another was to sit in on cable traffic and get a sense of the exciting world he was being denied.

What Egypt needed, thought Corcoran, as he read the inquiry from Israel, was a coup, engineered from without and putting a pro-Western soldier in power. That type of operation had been a CIA specialty in the fifties, like Iran and Guatemala. But today the world was different. The American people were different, too, more sophisticated about government affairs, more critical. The secret agencies had to watch themselves with Congress, and Watergate was reaching right into Director Helms's files. At Langley the corridors were filled with people hearing footsteps, those of outraged senators and their aides, brandishing subpoenas. In the old days . . .

Corcoran chuckled as he read the lines about the Nazi menace. As a gentile he found it difficult to appreciate Israel's paranoia about Eichmann and the others. As a realist he had little time to waste on contemplation of a Fourth Reich springing up. But he picked up the phone and asked for the South American desk. When Carlo Menderes answered, Corcoran said: "Only because I'm an incurable romantic, what's the latest rundown on the old Nazi leaders? Are they living it up in Buenos Aires or what?"

Carlo was anxious to show his expertise.

"Señor Corcoran, I am the reigning expert on the lives of German exiles. Our files are updated to nineteen sixty-five on the suspects. Bormann never left Europe. As you perhaps read, they just identified his bones in Berlin. Mengele lives in the jungles of Brazil. Sometimes he crosses into Paraguay to see a girlfriend. Who else?"

"I don't know. You tell me."

"Who cares. They're scattered around the continent, they have some money from stolen treasure, they're old men with fading dreams or none. Every once in a while, a historian or sometimes a Jewish organization asks us for information but we have a dead file on this thing. They don't matter anymore."

"Thanks, Carlo, I'm sorry I asked. But at least I can sleep better tonight. That's something."

LANGLEY TO U.S. EMBASSY: TEL AVIV—LAWTON OUR

OPINION NO POSSIBLE CONNECTION WITH NAZI
INVOLVEMENT. TELL YOUR CONTACT TO KEEP EYES ON
KREMLIN NOT BERCHTESGADEN. CIAO.

CORCORAN

6

The man with the crescent-shaped scar over his left eye
passed quickly through customs at the Rio airport and
drove away in a chauffeured car. In the back seat he leaned
against the upholstery and tried to unwind. The flight had
been pleasant enough, but Johannes Richter was nearing
the end of his endurance. At sixty-three he looked trim,
but Richter knew how deceptive that was. A battery of
doctors in Paraguay had given him the bad news in
October, just before he left for Tokyo.

They found a tumor the size of a pea imbedded in a fold
of his cerebellum. The prognosis: surgical excision
offered him a reasonable chance of survival, though he
faced partial paralysis and loss of certain cerebral func-
tions. Left to grow, the malignancy would kill him in
about a year, fifteen months at the most. Already Richter
was having moments of dizziness and, at times, flashes of
light blurred his vision. But in rejecting surgery he had
made a conscious choice and was not unhappy with it.
Either way he would eventually be useless to the cause he
served and his masters needed him now.

"They're with us." The chauffeur was staring beyond
Richter through the rear-view mirror.

"Don't worry, Gunter. They were bound to catch up
with me sooner or later. I'm surprised it took so long."

Richter did not bother to turn and look at the blue Fiat
trailing him along the superhighway into the Brazilian
interior.

Gunter slipped a revolver onto the seat beside him as he nervously dialed the radio for some music. Richter opened a briefcase and took out a batch of papers.

"Relax, I said. The Shin Bet just wants to know where I'm going. They won't harm us. Otherwise I'd have been dead years ago."

He began reading the top sheet. Neatly typed, it bore the letterhead of the West German Defense Ministry.

On June 22, 1973, the subject presented new demands. Instead of fifty thousand dollars American, she now insists on three payments totaling two hundred thousand dollars, to be deposited in a specified subway locker in East Berlin. Subject claims her life has been threatened repeatedly by agents of the Brandt government and therefore any prior agreements are meaningless. The Chancellor's reaction has not yet been ascertained but it seems likely he will ask us to meet her requirements, especially since any hint of scandal will certainly topple the fragile coalition he has formed with the opposition party.

Our problem is to decide whether we can continue our arrangement with subject. The possibility of unlimited tapping of our secret budget emerges, since appetites in such blackmail cases are seldom satisfied. At a certain point we must discuss the feasibility of cutting off both subject and victim.

Richter smiled to himself as he riffled the papers and came to another note, this one handwritten, from the foreign office.

Chancellor's mood verges on despondent. Magazines and newspapers question his ability to continue in office

as he seems close to breakdown over fading prospects for
European unity and collateral detente with Brezhnev.

In different handwriting at the bottom, someone had remarked: "How touching. If they only knew the real reasons for his mood."

The chauffeur had turned left off the highway and headed south into the grassy farmland of the Mato Grasso. Behind them the blue Fiat swiftly moved into line and assumed its stalking position, three hundred yards back on the flat stretch of road.

Richter still ignored the Israelis. He even felt a certain twinge of pride that they were devoting so much time to him. For eleven years now they had watched him, ever since he had come out of the jungle and taken up open residence in an apartment house in Asunción. Then he had been nervous because Eichmann had just been hanged, but the Brotherhood council felt world opinion had damaged the Jews in that episode and he could safely emerge to test the situation. And it had been right. The Shin Bet locked onto him immediately. His rooms were searched. Agents followed him into restaurants, photographed him, read his mail. But they never harmed him, preferring to watch, screen his acquaintances, and uncover the network that supported him.

For eleven years Richter ran an import-export business, which allowed him to travel freely to Europe and the United States. He never met with old friends from the Brotherhood and never attempted to elude his pursuers, who sat on the same planes and slept at the same hotels he did.

When he left home again in November, the Shin Bet faithfully tracked him to Tokyo. It was only on the return trip, in Beirut, that Richter changed the rules, suddenly bolting away from his lulled antagonists and disappearing in the direction of Algiers. For eight months he eluded them, doubling back and forth across continents, until finally back in South America, he had accomplished all his assigned duties.

The document now in his hands was a NATO top-secret report, which presented an analysis of the current American political scene:

Ambassadors from all countries flooding cable traffic with same basic theme: White House in state of complete chaos result of Watergate probe. From Oval Office to State Department, no one making responsible decisions on major issues. Nixon fast losing support of electorate as daily admissions of guilt from subordinates erode his credibility. Neither he nor Kissinger paying much attention to European situation, which causes growing discontent and fear in Common Market countries . . .

"We're here," Gunter said, and Richter stopped reading as they pulled up beside a Paraná river dock, where an old ferryboat was blowing a whistle to announce its departure. The car drove up the ramp and into the oily stench of the ship's interior. As Gunter and Richter got out, they saw the Fiat idling on the dock, and the two occupants talking to each other.

"If they come on, alert the captain. He'll take care of it," Richter said as he walked to the stairs leading to the upper deck. "I need a breath of air."

By the time he reached the railing and held onto it for a moment to stop his dizziness, the Fiat had pulled on board and the ferry was moving out into the current.

About twenty passengers were aboard, natives dressed in white campesino clothes, topped by straw sombreros. They lounged at the rails, gazing at the jungle growth now crowding in on them from the shore. No one paid any attention to Johannes Richter, who was breathing deeply of the fragrances from the luxurious foliage.

The boat ride took over an hour, to a spot where the river narrowed to less than a hundred yards. Another dock loomed on the right and the ferry maneuvered clumsily about, pushing in gingerly to disembark its cargo. Richter went back down to the car, where Gunter revved the engine and waited impatiently while the gate was lowered and banged onto the dock.

"You informed the captain?"

"Yes, sir," Gunter answered, pointing to the rear. The Fiat was there, but the Israelis had disappeared and a native now sat in the driver's seat.

As Gunter drove slowly up the ramp and onto the dock, Richter turned to see a group of men crowding the rail at the stern of the ferry. They were lifting something high and then bodies fell, one by one, into the water. And at that moment the boat reversed engines and the propeller screws passed noisily over the spot where the Israeli agents had fallen into the shallow water.

Gunter pulled ahead as Richter returned again to his reading. Ten minutes later, the car bumped onto a dirt road and proceeded a few more miles inland. On either side the jungle seemed nearly impenetrable and then suddenly they were in a huge cleared area and Richter saw the pink hacienda on the right, ringed by a wire fence.

At the gate, Gunter got out and spoke briefly to the guard, who made a phone call to the main house. In moments, an old man came down the path toward the visitors. Dressed in a loose-fitting peasant shirt and black pants tucked into shiny boots, he was waving at Richter, who walked toward him. It had been eleven years since they had seen each other and Richter noticed his friend seemed to have lost none of the aggressive manner he always had. His once bull-like neck did look somewhat shriveled; his hair, though still close cropped against the skull, was starkly white. The mole on his cheek stood out more noticeably against the wrinkled skin.

When the man reached Richter, he embraced him affectionately: "It went well, I hear." He spoke in a Bavarian dialect.

"It went perfectly. We're just about ready now."

The main gate clanged shut behind them as they walked arm in arm into the hacienda.

7

For several weeks curious Germans had noticed the passage across the land of the fledgling politician Karl Radel. Increasingly vocal as he appeared at rallies and political picnics, the hook-nosed lawyer was quickly establishing a position to the right of Chancellor Willy Brandt. Insistently badgering the government for its lenient policies toward the Communist bloc, Radel now attracted crowds of bellicose sympathizers who punctuated his deliberately subdued speeches with shouts of approval. Twice already, clashes had occurred between these followers and bands of student protesters waving Communist placards and singing the Internationale. But police had always quelled the riots before anyone was seriously injured, and thus they had gone virtually unnoticed in the press.

And now, on a sticky August evening, Karl Radel was driving past the darkened bulk of the Gothic Cologne Cathedral, past the Hotel Dom, and on to an auditorium where hundreds of people had gathered to listen to him discuss Germany's role in Western European affairs. The crowd was friendly and attentive, and as Radel was introduced by the chairman, they cheered for several minutes.

When he waved them to silence and began to speak it was obvious that he had decided to drop his calm manner, his careful but cautious criticism of Brandt and other German figures.

''. . . What is wrong with us, the descendants of

Bismarck, that we allow ourselves to be manipulated by men who grovel before the enemy? What kind of people are we now that we let nations that bombed us and invaded our land continue to dominate our lives?''

The crowd was hushed. Some people looked uneasily about to gauge reactions, then turned back to the podium, where Radel was waving his fist.

''For nearly thirty years we have been mongrelized by the troops of conquering nations. The Americans, the British, the French have all tried to keep us down, to divide us. And yet with all that, look at the miracle. West Germany is number three in the world in gross national product, the acknowledged leader of the Common Market. And behind that wall in East Germany, our brothers, and they are still our brothers . . .''

Several listeners were on their feet, yelling agreement, and suddenly hundreds of Germans rose up with an animal growl that brought chills to the spine.

''Even they have conquered their tormentors and are number nine in the world in gross national product . . .''

The roar was there again, a frenzied, sustained outburst, as though suppressed for years and now spouting forth from frustrated hearts and minds.

At the back of the hall, a lone cameraman snapped pictures of the scene in quick succession, dodging from one spot to another as the huge hall rocked to the beginning strains of the German anthem, ''Deutschland, Deutschland, uber alles.''

Radel stepped back, his face flushed with excitement. He mopped his forehead with a white handkerchief and smiled down at his audience, whose long-suppressed passions he had unlocked. Ushers had begun moving through the aisles, begging the demonstrators to keep quiet, and then suddenly it was hushed again and Radel continued:

36

"Germany must not be afraid to assert itself in the world of nations. We must reassume our rightful role, for we have earned that honor. The millions who died in the last war are crying out to you for vengeance. It is our sacred duty to them . . ."

The front door to the auditorium crashed in and a jumble of police and civilians burst through in a welter of swinging fists and clubs. Screams of women were drowned out by the curses of rioters, the sudden, sharp sound of revolver shots. In seconds, Karl Radel's sympathizers were part of the mob, breaking seats, tearing clothes, and spilling their blood.

Radel did not stay to witness the riot. Ducking offstage and out a side door, he ran into the street, where hundreds of people had locked in a reeling embrace with each other and helmeted police. Radel jumped into his car, strategically positioned for a quick getaway, and sped away from the battlefield.

In a nearby gutter lay the cameraman who had been taking photos inside the hall. His mouth bleeding from a blow by an unseen attacker, his camera smashed beyond repair, he struggled to his feet and leaned against a wall. In the distance the sound of sirens signaled the arrival of reinforcements to cope with the savage fighting at the hall. But in his daze, the photographer, a Shin Bet agent, heard only the words to the Communist Internationale, rising to a crescendo in the streets of Cologne.

Less than a week later, more than one hundred and fifty miles to the south, the duty officer at the U.S. Army ammunition dump near Bad Nauheim was almost at the end of his four to midnight shift. His was a lonely job, commanding a ten-man group guarding a series of corrugated steel warehouses holding ordnance supplies for the Seventh Army. At sundown, traffic at the dump slowed to a trickle and after ten, the place was virtually lifeless.

At eleven-thirty his phone rang and a sergeant at the front gate told him a convoy of five trucks had just pulled up, requesting permission to enter.

"What the hell do they want at this hour? I don't have anything scheduled in until morning."

"I don't know, Lieutenant. They have papers signed by the quartermaster in Heidelberg to pick up one thousand AR-fifteens, ten thousand rounds of ammo, and a thousand grenades. The orders are stamped as of twelve noon today."

"Okay, hold them there. I'll be right over."

The officer stubbed out his cigarette, put on his field jacket, and walked out into the compound. When he reached the gate he found the sergeant joking with the convoy leader, a captain, who returned the duty officer's salute and said:

"Hansberry from Ninth Division, Lieutenant. I'm sorry we're so late but the last truck in line broke down on the autobahn and we had to limp along."

He was smiling apologetically and the duty officer found it hard to be mad. "That's okay. It's just you should have called in from the road so we'd have a crew to load you up."

"Don't worry about that. My guys can help you out."

Hansberry handed over his papers and the duty officer stepped inside a little shack to read them in better light. Each slip was signed properly by a Colonel Collins, whom he knew; each manifest had been countersigned by Henshaw in Heidelberg.

"But where's the motor pool release for your vehicles?" the duty officer called just as a slug from a silencer-equipped .45 ripped into his head and smashed his body to the floor. Captain Hansberry stood over him for a moment and then whirled to see the sergeant running frantically toward a warehouse door. The captain fired three time and the sergeant seemed to leave the ground for a moment before collapsing limply into a row of manicured bushes.

Telling two of his men to hide the corpses, Hansberry jumped into the lead truck and led the convoy directly over to Building 4, unguarded by the skeleton crew and only fitfully lit by a searchlight. In less than forty minutes the trucks had been loaded and Hansberry led them back through the main gate. As he passed the sentry shack, a trickle of blood oozed down the steps onto the ground.

The theft at Bad Nauheim was just one of four such crimes committed the same night. American CID agents and West German intelligence people combined to track down the plotters who executed these raids. In three weeks they found not a single worthwhile clue and in desperation Army Intelligence called for help.

CORCORAN, LANGLEY
SUGGEST SITUATION HERE IN YOUR BALLPARK. ALL SIGNS POINT TO SOVIET INVOLVEMENT.
                              BURNS G-2 MANNHEIM

Reprieved at last by weary superiors, Matt Corcoran kissed Tessa goodbye at Dulles airport. His wife could hardly recognize the change in him. Freshly shaved, splashed with an English cologne, he looked like a prosperous businessman in his well-pressed chocolate-brown suit. In a few days, she knew, his clothes would be as wrinkled and sloppy as ever, but for a moment she beamed on him like a doting mother sending a son off to church. Then he was gone and Tessa went back to her lonely world, the only one she could ever have with such a man.

Corcoran arrived in Heidelberg on September 20 and immediately sought out the investigators who were still baffled by the breaks. No witnesses had remained alive to identify the invaders. At Kaiserslautern, Mannheim, Hanau, and Bad Nauheim, they had killed a total of seven men to prevent discovery.

Corcoran was furious.

"You mean to tell me some lousy Krauts could stick up four ammo dumps, knock over a huge supply of ordnance, and disappear into the fog without a trace?"

"Yes, sir. It seems our security was not prepared for such a thing. It never happened before and we just hadn't planned on anything so professional."

"Bullshit!"

"And then you know since Vietnam, we've had to cut back on manpower and the soldiers don't give a damn over here. Half of them are on dope . . ."

Corcoran was out of the room and on his way to lunch. At the Graf Zeppelin hotel his guest was waiting for him and they greeted each other with obvious warmth. Heinrich Muller had long been engaged in counterespionage work for the West German government and Corcoran admired his thorough, Teutonic approach to investigations.

"We've got a funny one here, Kamerad." He shrugged at the monocled agent. "I'm embarrassed at my own army for letting it happen. Those damn fools at the Pentagon . . ."

"It's all part of something else, I'm afraid." The German's English was good, but heavily accented. His mood was suddenly grim and he shook his head warily.

"Matthew, things have changed a bit since you were here last. Brandt seems to be in trouble with Moscow and East Berlin. And after all he was doing to work it out with them."

Corcoran had ordered a bourbon on the rocks and he almost gulped it down as he listened to Muller brief him.

"Yeah, everyone has told Willy to get rid of that guy but he won't for some damn reason."

"Guillaume is just one. Even my boss is on the list of suspects. They say he's been working for the East bloc for years."

"Jesus!" Corcoran ordered another drink while Muller toyed with a light Moselle.

"But we know that's rot. It's just another part of the line being pushed from Moscow. They're up to something big and Brandt's in the middle."

"Then what about these ammo dump robberies?"

Muller had a theory. "If you're trying to overthrow a government, why not arm the people in the streets?"

"But damn it, the Commies have been working detente with Brandt for years now. Why in hell would they want a revolution in Bonn?"

"And then there's the woman they have working on the Chancellor. You know they infiltrated her, and now she's about to bankrupt the budget of the intelligence service. We've got a terrible problem keeping that one quiet."

Corcoran was doodling on the tablecloth, a flowery pattern, curly petals, all neatly interlaced around a triangular bud.

"KGB, Fourth Directorate," he muttered, and Muller

agreed, adding: "Probably the Disinformation Section. They play chess with us all the time and this time they're four or five moves ahead."

Corcoran suddenly knew what he had to do. Draining his second bourbon, he jumped up and excused himself. "Heinrich, you've lost a free lunch but I'll mark you down on my expense account anyway."

As he walked out the door, Muller signaled to a man sitting alone in a corner. The stranger joined him and Muller broke into a grin that revealed two gold teeth.

"Just tell Radel the Cold War may be about to heat up again."

8

To Matt Corcoran the problem in Germany clearly displayed traces of a master hand at work. After fifteen years, a familiar hand. He decided to deal directly with the architect.

At the reception desk of the Soviet Embassy in Bad Godesberg, he handed the secretary his card.

"Dmitri Polchak, your press officer, please. Tell him I know his boss."

When Polchak appeared, he was stiff and unfriendly.

"Mr. Corcoran, you have me at a disadvantage. I don't know you but you say you know my superior."

"Shame on you, Polchak. You damn well know me and I know you. KGB, last in Cyprus, maintaining a direct link with Soviet ships in the Mediterranean. Before that, Peru, arming rebels in the hills around Lima. But never mind the history lesson. I didn't come here to show you how smart I was. I want to see Glasov."

Polchak's hands fumbled for his glasses and he tried to cover his confusion by slowly cleaning them with a handkerchief.

"Mr. Corcoran, I'm afraid you're wrong on two counts. First about my activities and, second, I have no idea who this man Glasov is."

"All right, Polchak," Corcoran sighed. "Let's stop the act. Mikhail Mikhailovich Glasov has been my friend for more than fifteen years. In the Belgian Congo, he and I worked together against the Chinese agents. Remember that one? I'm sure you learned that operation by heart at school. Since then Glasov has gotten a big job at the Center in Moscow and he runs you and other agents here in Germany and France. How's that?''

Polchak was impassive.

''And,'' Corcoran probed Polchak in the chest, ''he happens to be Brezhnev's special pet. So if you don't get in touch with him for me you may wind up running a butcher shop in Irkutsk.''

Dmitri Polchak glared at the probing finger. His concern had turned to anger at the insolence of the American agent and he wanted to smash him in the face. But the thought of Glasov was with him as he turned and walked out to the cable machine.

Corcoran waited under a picture of Kosygin for more than an hour until Polchak finally came back and handed him a note.

''Fly Aeroflot 192 Berlin Saturday night. Will meet you. Glasov.''

Corcoran pocketed the paper, pushed past Polchak to the door, and slammed it on the Russian's reddening face.

The dacha was in the Lenin Hills northwest of Moscow and it was beautifully furnished, elegant even, thought Matt Corcoran.

''Mike, you've really come a long way since we slept in those damn trees in the Congo.''

Mikhail Glasov roared and grabbed Corcoran in a bear hug. He was a huge man, at least two hundred and fifty pounds, and his arms were like oak trees as he swung his bulky victim in the air. ''I can't believe you are really here, in my house. Nadia, come here," and Glasov's wife slipped into the room and stood shyly beside him.

"This man saved my life once so you owe him a kiss and a drink." She was blushing brightly, a pretty blond woman, getting stout like her husband and yet trying to salvage something of her youthful figure.

"We'll be up all night, babushka, so don't worry if you hear glasses breaking."

Nadia shook her head in reproach. "Mikhail, you'll die of vodka poisoning." When he laughed again, she turned to Corcoran. "The kiss you have and welcome," and she pecked Matt on the cheek. "The drink he'll give you for sure."

As she left, Glasov looked after her fondly. "I guess we both have to have understanding women in our business. Thank God for that."

"Watch yourself, comrade. The walls are listening."

"Not here. Downtown yes, but they don't follow me here. And anyway I sweep the place everyday."

From a cabinet he pulled out a bottle and held it high.

"Jack Daniels, right! Just off the plane from New York."

Glasov was almost childlike as he poured out a huge tumblerful for Corcoran. "So now let's drink to us," and the two men clinked glasses solemnly.

For an hour they talked of the past, of the Congo and the complicated plans they had hatched to thwart Maoist spies trying to inspire revolution. The money for the scheme came from the NATO budget in Paris. The untraceable weapons were issued from Moscow. When the Chinese had been killed or scattered, the two spies parted and disappeared back into the shadow world of intelligence. But they always kept track of each other and at odd moments communicated: a postcard, a phone call, sometimes greetings through embassy personnel. Despite their devotion to different ideologies, Corcoran and Glasov continued a friendship forged in a jungle.

"But you came all this way for an argument, I think, Matt. Your Irish face has lost a little of its charm."

Into his third bourbon by now, Corcoran was already past any diplomatic approach. "Mikhail Mikhailovich, you are one dumb Russian."

Glasov smiled tolerantly. "Nothing's changed. You never waste words."

"No, not when I smell a rat. Your bureau has gone crazy with this German brainstorm."

"What are you talking about? We don't have anything big going on there right now."

"Wrong. It's just like France in 1968 when you finally got rid of De Gaulle. Same tactics, same basic plan. Undermine the people's faith in the leader, riots in the streets, anarchy."

"Thanks for the compliment on De Gaulle, Matt. That was a gem. But you're crazy about the German thing. You talk about riots in the streets. You must mean the funny things that happen when Radel makes a speech. And the ammo dump raids. And the spy Guillaume in Brandt's office. Now there I've got you. For three years we've tried to make the East Germans get him out of there. But they won't listen and we don't want to crack down on them too hard. It's a new approach from the Presidium."

Glasov busied himself refilling the drinks and then stuffed himself with black bread and little meats while Corcoran worked himself up into a rage.

"Damn it, Mike, you've even got that mistress of Brandt's nailing him for money. Now what the hell am I supposed to think about that? She'll squeeze him dry or go

46

tell her story to the papers. And then he's out and you have one more leader to hang from your belt. Don't tell me the KGB is innocent on this. And what I don't understand is why do you want to finish Brandt off? For Christ's sake, every time I pick up a paper, he's swimming in the Black Sea with Brezhnev.''

''That's just the point, Matthew. If you really think about it, there's no percentage in that for us.''

''Unless you have another handpicked Chancellor in the wings who's ready to sell NATO down the river for some deutschemarks.''

''No, no, no.'' Glasov was being indulgent with his irate guest. ''Have some more food.'' He passed the tray to Corcoran, who picked up several hors d'oeuvres and chewed them slowly as he tried to gauge Glasov's sincerity.

''Look, you failed to mention the one possibility some of your own allies believe. We spoke of this Radel, the lawyer going around giving tough speeches. Do you know who he is? Have you been in touch yet with the Shin Bet?''

''No, goddamn it, I've been locked up in Langley for a year.''

''I know that, but the Israelis must have contacted your people about him.''

''I got a cable from Tel Aviv a while ago, not about Radel, but asking for information on Nazis in the Middle East. We just laughed it off because we don't have a thing in our files on them.''

''Shame on the CIA,'' Glasov chuckled, as Corcoran ignored the jibe. ''Anyway, are you saying the Shin Bet is chasing after someone like Radel while their country is surrounded by Arabs? Why look for old bogeymen at a time like this?''

"Come on, Matt, you know the Shin Bet better than that. They can handle both jobs nicely. And they think Radel is really someone else, a man they've looked for as long as they have for Bormann. We think they're on the right track."

Corcoran now showed guarded interest. His belligerence had evaporated and he seemed almost deferential as he asked:

"Who is he?"

"A killer named August Bleemer."

"Never heard of him."

"Well, we have a section in the KGB which keeps a file on wanted men from World War II. Silly, you think, but then you didn't know the SS. Anyway, when this Radel or Bleemer surfaced, to make a political name for himself, we checked him and found nothing, at first. But we kept digging in a special way and believe we found an answer."

"Like what?"

"That is my surprise for you." Glasov pulled Corcoran out of the chair and pushed him toward a bedroom. "Go to bed now. And in a few days I'll show you one of our top secrets. How's that for being an old friend?"

9

The heat was stultifying, draining the energy of those who worked in its intensity. But for Horst Clemens, Cairo's humidity was like a tonic, especially after all those years in Russian prison camps, where he had dug coal in twenty-below-zero weather. That was his continual nightmare. The perspiration that stained his clothes at eight A.M. every day in Egypt was salutary compared to the sharp pains that once invaded his bones on the Siberian plains.

The German war hero had been in Egypt for four months. During that period he plunged into his favorite pastime, the study of waging war. From the moment he understood the nature of his new job, Clemens devoted his entire time to the problem. While Egyptian officers made excuses and went off to officers' clubs for drinks and gambling, he stayed at his desk, bending his rusty mind to a staggering task: transporting two mechanized armies across the Suez Canal, in the heat of battle.

For weeks he immersed himself in the latest technology of modern warfare. Gone were the Mark IIIs and IVs from the days of the panzers; now he dealt with Soviet T-62s, incredible armored vehicles. Gone were the 88mm guns which the German army once used to terrorize the world. In their place he studied highly sophisticated Russian surface-to-air missiles, SAMs, which Clemens had only read about and now had to integrate into his calculations.

Within two months of arriving he had devised a precise plan. For the rest of the time he badgered everyone at the war ministry to speed up their own timetables, to follow his blueprint so nothing would go wrong.

Now Clemens felt ready. His years of training in the Wehrmacht had not been wasted and despite vast changes in technology, the basic fundamentals of fording bodies of water had not altered. As he relaxed in his room at an army base east of Cairo, Clemens took time out to write a letter:

Liebchen:
We have finished our latest revisions in the project. I feel so good about myself because people say I lend a touch of genius to their endeavor. After all this time it makes me thank God I was given another opportunity to prove myself.
How is everything going? I miss you very much and hope the situation here will be cleared up shortly . . . so we can take our walks again in the park . . .

In Washington, D.C., the monthly interagency intelligence briefing had just gotten under way at the Executive Office Building near the White House.

"Ladies and gentlemen, the evidence is in and unmistakably clear." The speaker was standing before a map of the Middle East. "Here," he said, jabbing at Egypt, "they're moving their armies to the Suez at night. Here," pointing at Syria, "we have a buildup of tanks and artillery that can only be described as awesome. And in Damascus at the moment, the airport is jammed with Soviet personnel booking passage out on every commercial airliner."

Morrow from Defense asked: "What about the Egyptian air force?"

"Gone from its normal fields around Cairo. All fighter

squadrons have been moved west to the Libyan border or in some cases into Libya."

"And Gaddafi? What's his role in this?"

"That man is still calling every day for war with Zionism so nothing has changed with him. It's Sadat we have to worry about, he and Assad in Syria. They've met at least twice in recent weeks and then there's that curious trip Sadat took to see Faisal in Riyadh."

Smoke from a dozen cigarettes and pipes curled upward as the group contemplated this nugget of information.

"Now this problem is different from last time," the speaker continued. "In nineteen sixty-seven, the Arabs were disorganized, squabbling with each other, and the Israelis wiped them out. But Sadat learned a big lesson then and it's quite probable he's decided to attack across the Suez while holding a trump card he negotiated with his rich colleagues."

"An oil boycott?" several voices chimed together.

"Nothing but! If he can get across the canal and hold on, all signs point to the Arabs finally presenting a united front against the industrial world. Either negotiate with us for a return of our land or face economic disaster."

"Can they get across?" asked a lady from State.

"I don't see how but that depends a lot on what the Israelis know and decide to do. If they catch on or we tell them what we know, there's no question they'll launch another preventive strike. But even then, Sadat will call on the sheiks for an oil embargo to drive the Israelis back."

"What if we don't tell them?" Morrow from Defense asked what was on everybody's mind.

"Simple. Either they'll still attack first or Sadat will. If the Israelis strike, we'll certainly get hit with the embargo. But if Sadat attacks first, he must get across the canal

51

before the Arab states can feel cocky enough to face down the West with a boycott.''

''Then let's play it cool,'' Morrow said. ''If we don't give the Israelis any info that might push them into a preemptive attack, Sadat might get cold feet on his own and cancel any war plans. That way the oil still flows.''

The conference broke into a babble of conflicting opinions as analysts and agents tried to reach a common approach.

Two hours later, their monthly intelligence recommendations went to the White House for scrutiny. Uppermost on the list was an urgent appeal to the President not to alarm Israeli leaders with data that might precipitate a war alert and its fatal consequences.

No matter how careful the security was, Egyptian planners could not completely muffle the roar of tank divisions approaching the west bank of the Suez Canal. They came in clockwork precision, on a schedule worked out over months. Organizational procedures were astounding, far different from previous wars, and by nightfall of Yom Kippur the armor was all in place, hidden under netting, surrounded by trucks, guns, supplies, and thousands of soldiers burrowed into the loose sand of the desert.

On the east bank, a thin line of Israelis watched, listened, and reported back that the Egyptians were ready. And in a stucco house in Tel Aviv, maps were being dotted with colored flags, not only in the canal area, but in the Golan Heights, where for days Syrian forces had been inching forward to jumping-off positions. The latest ominous word from Damascus was the arrival of a squadron of Russian TU-22 fighter-bombers, a weapons system never before introduced into the Middle East.

In the same stucco house, Moshe Dayan paced the floor in the ague of a man torn by indecision. His instincts told him to strike at the enemy immediately and yet he knew the problems being faced by Golda Meir as she argued with the rest of her cabinet over the cruel prospects for her country. Her discussions raged into the early morning of Yom Kippur, and while thousands of Israeli citizens sought spiritual succor in synagogues, Mrs. Meir sat in her own kitchen with men from the Knesset and tried to read the Arabs' minds. Distracted, she barely remembered to have someone cancel a visit she planned to her sister on a kibbutz. Then she and her friends went over the incontrovertible proof of a major enemy buildup on the frontiers. A crucial question arose: "What does American intelligence estimate?" The answer came from an air force officer: "Just another in a series of maneuvers by enemy forces. SR-seventy-one reconnaissance planes detect no activity indicating actual war footing."

Unwilling to begin another preventive war for fear of world condemnation, Premier Meir made a fateful compromise. She issued a partial alert, and across the nation reserves were called from religious services to report to their units. As they scrambled away the October sun shone straight down on the golden Dome of the Rock in Jerusalem, on the choppy blue gulf at Haifa, and the barren rocks around Sharm El Sheik. But it was already too late for hundreds of Israeli troops standing in the front lines. A drumfire bombardment began at two P.M. and from the west bank of the Suez Canal a miracle unfolded. Engineers began to push five bridges, breakaway, and easily transportable, into the water, linking them in seg-

53

ments to form a path across the canal into the Sinai. When Israeli fighters pounced on them, they met utter defeat, for in a marvel of technological inventiveness the Egyptians wed the SAM missiles to the fording of a body of water. Swarms of the heat-seekers rose into the sky and destroyed most of the attackers. The rest of the Israeli Mirages and Phantoms fled to the safety of their own airfields.

Horst Clemens's bridges held that day and would hold through all the succeeding days.

10

Camp Yelabuga lay on the immense Russian tundra, northeast of Moscow and just below the Arctic Circle. It had been there since 1923, when Nikolai Lenin had it built along with hundreds of other slave-labor centers. As part of what was later known as the Gulag Archipelago, it housed many of the millions of Soviet citizens who incurred the wrath of the state. For more than twenty years Yelabuga remained a detention area; the tundra around it filled with the ashes of its victims. But in 1943, its role changed as thousands of German prisoners of war jammed its fetid barracks. Many died in the first months from starvation and neglect. Those who were left chopped wood in nearby forests and worked coal mines in the neighborhood for long years. By 1950 most of the survivors were repatriated home.

Five years later, the Chancellor of the new West German government, Konrad Adenauer, went to Moscow and pleaded with Nikita Khrushchev to release any POWs left in jail. In a violent argument before witnesses at a diplomatic reception, the Russian Premier denounced the murderers still held within Soviet borders:

"In the Soviet Union there are only war criminals of the former Hitler armies—criminals that were convicted by a Soviet court for especially grave crimes . . . against peace and humanity. . . . They are men who have lost the human countenance; they are men guilty of atrocity, of arson, of murder committed against women, children and old people . . ."

His face contorted with rage, Khrushchev sputtered on: "The Soviet people cannot forget the capital crimes committed by these criminal elements, as, for instance, the shooting of seventy thousand men in Kiev on the Babi Yar. We cannot forget these million people who were killed, gassed, and burned to death. Can anyone forget the tons of hair that were cut off from women who were tortured to death. Those . . . on our side have witnessed all that happened in Maidenek. In the Maidenek and Auschwitz camps more than five and a half million people, all innocent, were murdered . . . I could name the concentration camps in Smolensk, Krasnodar, Stavropol . . . Novgorod, Kaunas—where hundreds of thousands of Soviet citizens were tortured to death; we cannot forget the scorched towns and villages. . . . And the men I mentioned are criminals who committed these monstrous crimes."

Adenauer stood patiently, not wilting under the attack. When Khrushchev paused, still furious, the Chancellor asked him politely to establish a new era of friendship between nations. He pleaded for the Soviet Union to forget its rancor at admitted outrages and allow the prisoners to go home.

Within forty-eight hours, the German leader stood before a battery of microphones at a Moscow press conference and announced a great diplomatic victory.

". . . The Soviet government—Mr. Bulganin and Mr. Khrushchev—expressly declared during the negotiations that the Soviet Union has no longer any German prisoners of war, but only convicted war criminals—as they put it.

"All of them will leave the Soviet Union in the very near future . . ."

Adenauer was wrong. While more than nine thousand German officers and men did begin the long journey back to freedom, the Russians selected the most notorious men they kept in captivity and herded them across Russia to Yelabuga, where early snows had begun and temperatures were reaching toward zero.

When repatriated German prisoners of war reached home, they warned government officials that some of their friends had been spirited away at the last minute. And when West German officials complained to the Kremlin that their bargain had not been kept, that many Nazi soldiers were unaccounted for, the Russians told them they were just trying to fan the flames of the Cold War, that all German war criminals had been released.

The issue remained closed as the world turned to more pressing problems.

But at Yelabuga, the Soviet KGB now assumed direct responsibility for more than two thousand POWs, the dregs of the Nazi system, who had personally confessed to the deaths of more than four million human beings. For these sadists, the Russians reserved special attention as a means of expiation to those who had fallen during the Second World War.

Eighteen years had passed at Yelabuga when Matt Corcoran found himself looking into a ravine where more than a hundred men stared up at guards lining the rim. They were shivering, though the weather was mild, and their faces were strangely passive, devoid of normal feelings, as their captors raised rifles and pointed them down into the pit.

"Look at them," Glasov was saying, "tough bastards, no doubt about it."

Corcoran suddenly realized that not one of the victims

was under fifty; most were much older. Balding or silver-haired, they formed a loose military parade formation, it seemed, and stood patiently waiting for the inevitable.

"Fire," came the command and several hundred bullets thudded into the ground, raising puffs of dirt, ricocheting away except for some that smashed into bone and flesh and left three men writhing on the valley floor.

As "Cease fire" rang out, a whimpering cry rose from the ravine and an old man was on his hands and knees, pawing at the ground, pressing his face into the grass to hide. He was screaming now, something unintelligible to those on top, and the guards were making their way down the slope to check the wounded.

The camp commandant whispered to Glasov: "That one is no good to us anymore," pointing to the hysterical one. When Glasov shrugged, the officer hollered something to a guard, who walked down the cliff wall, marched past the survivors, and stood over the one who had lost his sanity. As the man raised his face in supplication, the Russian shot him behind the right ear.

"You see, Matt, we try to keep these men healthy as long as possible. Otherwise there's no point in having this camp at all." Glasov was explaining Yelabuga over lunch an hour later. "Take a drink or something. You look a little green."

Corcoran had seen death and torture for years but the shock of this camp numbed him as he tried to understand the rationale for it.

"We lost twenty million dead in that war and those men you saw helped run the extermination plan."

"But that was nearly thirty years ago, Mike. Even you have to admit this place is barbaric."

"We call it a retribution center. For my part, I think of

58

my sister every time I come here. The Nazis put her in one of their Doll Houses in Kiev and when they finished with her, hung her from a lamppost." Glasov stopped eating and his eyes clouded with tears. "She was beautiful, Matt, but not when I cut her down.

"Our only purpose is to make these men live long enough to pay them back for the slaughter of so many innocents," Glasov went on. "And to that end we approached the problem as scientifically as possible. Each prisoner has a diet guaranteed to sustain him. Each prisoner is examined by a psychiatrist once a month to make sure he can reasonably endure psychological pressures applied to him. In that way we keep them functioning almost to their normal mortality span. Of course we lose some to accidents, and at times we eliminate some to keep the rest guessing about their own fate. Otherwise they might think we're kidding."

It was laid out for Corcoran in every clinical detail, and he marveled at its brutal efficiency. It was only when he saw the pathetic men at the ravine that he remembered the Russians were dealing with human beings, not statistics, and then the old faces that stared up haunted him.

"I know what you're thinking, we're as bad as they are to do this. Maybe you're right, but the people we have here are the worst of the lot. They killed for the sheer pleasure of it or because someone gave them lists and quotas. And that's why you're here, Matt, to meet one monster who may solve your problem in Germany."

As the sun faded through a grove of trees, Glasov and Corcoran mounted the stairs at the side of a concrete building and entered a small room where a window in the side wall provided a view that stunned the American. He was literally staring into the past, to 1943 and the

Holocaust. In a shower room, naked men crowded together under nozzles protruding from the ceiling. They were apprehensive, glancing up now and then, jostling each other. A few had already sat down to await the nightmare.

The commandant was beside Corcoran: "We copied this building directly from the Auschwitz plans. Every man down there was involved in gassing 'subhumans,' as they called us. Now what we do is herd them in here every two or three months. Sometimes we let them stand there for hours and then release them without any punishment. But today they get a taste."

Gas had begun to seep from the nozzles and the Germans moved away from it in a frantic mass, trying to seek a last moment of safety from the fumes. The white vapor now lay over them in a thick layer and some began to clutch their throats in agony. Then the retching began and the floor was soon slippery with vomit and excrement as muscles relaxed and the victims lost consciousness. In less than three minutes, the last German fell onto the pyramid of flesh and limbs.

"They're not dead, Mr. Corcoran," said the commandant. "This gas merely recreates the initial effects of Zyklon B, which they used in their own camps. The fight for breath, the nausea and panic. But they'll revive in a few minutes and then we let them lie in their filth for awhile. One or two are dead down there, I'm sure, from heart failure but that's good for the rest to remember."

Giant fans hummed through the building and the fumes slowly dissipated over the prostrate bodies. Glasov pointed. "In the middle there somewhere is the man you came to see. We'll bring him to you sometime tomorrow. I think after watching this you'll better understand what kind of person you'll be dealing with."

Corcoran and Glasov walked out into a twilight filled with a strong scent of flowers and the American breathed it in gratefully.

At five P.M. the next day, he watched Dieter Speck shambling across the yard. "That particular member of the species helped kill more than two hundred thousand 'defectives,' as his orders read. We caught him hiding in a cellar in Prague and have made his life miserable ever since. His immediate superior was none other than August Bleemer." Glasov had a triumphant look as he spoke.

Corcoran saw it all now. The Russians must have shown Speck a picture of Karl Radel, which he identified immediately as Bleemer.

"That's right. Hook-nosed Bleemer, easy to spot except that he left few witnesses and as far as we know no pictures. But one of our men in the Fourth Directorate met him in nineteen forty-four when he and Himmler visited barracks at Sobibor. He was sixteen years old, a slave laborer, and Bleemer passed within five feet of his bed. At the end of the war, everyone else in that barracks died, but my clerk lived because he burrowed under a fence and found a Polish family that kept him safe in an attic."

Speck had entered the office, standing stiffly upright in his striped gray uniform. Glasov's voice was pleasant, kindly. "Sit down," he said and handed the German a cigarette, which Speck accepted with a bow.

Corcoran was busy with mental addition. Eighteen years in Yelabuga, probably four or five times a year in the gas chamber, that made almost a hundred shower room ordeals, and here he was, amazingly healthy-looking and bright-eyed. Despite ill-fitting clothes and a pale complexion, Speck seemed at ease, neither broken nor subservient. His face was square, pockmarked, with a high forehead and black eyes that squinted without glasses. He kept dragging on the cigarette until Glasov asked: "Your age?"

"Fifty-eight, sir."

"Duties as an SS officer."

"Relocation and final solution of retarded and non-essential personnel."

Speck had dropped his cigarette into an ashtray and now reverted to his training.

"Your superior."

"Standartenfuhrer August Bleemer."

Glasov had been pacing the floor as he asked the questions, but he was now beside Speck, laying a hand on his shoulder.

"Tell us Bleemer's relationship to those in the Brotherhood."

"Herr Bleemer was to succeed Reichsleiter Bormann should the need arise."

"How well did you know Bleemer?"

"He was a second father to me." Corcoran watched Speck closely. He was staring straight ahead at a wall, his features blank, reciting for perhaps the thousandth time information the KGB had wrested from him over decades of interrogation.

Glasov sat down across from Speck and offered him another cigarette. "You're going home soon, Major."

Speck flinched slightly, but recovered quickly. "Yes, sir."

"And if you do what we tell you, you can buy a farm and live on it for the rest of your life."

Speck's hands clenched white but his face remained impassive. "Yes, sir."

"If you don't do what we say, those gas chamber visits will be child's play. Understand?"

"Yes, sir."

"This man will be your contact in Germany." Speck glanced briefly at Corcoran and nodded both greeting and acceptance.

"Now go and pack."

"Yes, sir." Dieter Speck rose swiftly, saluted, turned, and disappeared through the door.

"Bleemer's boy, Matt. He's the one who can find out what the hell is going on. If Bleemer is posing as Radel, he'll know and get close to him. And then it will all unravel."

Corcoran was at the window, checking the German's retreating figure. "Eighteen years of this and he's still sane. I'd have cracked wide open."

"That's because you're a sensitive Irishman, my friend. He's different. He's still proud of what he did to my people."

11

The sky over the desert was breathtakingly clear, with fields of stars glowing brightly over Horst Clemens's head. He was standing alone in front of a concrete block-house, once a command post for the Egyptian Third Army, but now Clemens's private home in the backwash of a war moved to the east. There, fitful flashes of gunfire marked the front line between his allies and the embattled Israelis, who had not yet recovered from the stunning coup inspired by Clemens's organizational genius. His bridges still spanned the canal; SAM missiles still provided superb protection against marauding Israeli jets. And across the bridges rolled thousands of tons of supplies for Egyptian forces now entrenched in the former Bar-Lev Line.

Clemens listened to the dull boom of artillery with satisfaction. It was a symphony he had almost forgotten, a mighty drumroll that spoke of power and relentless energy. It told of heroes and brave deeds in countless engagements and Clemens had always thrilled to its majesty.

At nine-thirty he went back inside the bunker to enjoy his final evening in Egypt. It was a small place, one room with a cot and footlocker in a corner; in the work area a desk had been covered with a white linen cloth, topped by a single plate, silverware, and a goblet. On a field stove a steak simmered and, after tending it, Clemens went to a tiny refrigerator and took out a bottle of Moët & Chandon, which he had bought in Cairo just for this occasion.

Although he was alone tonight, the German major always celebrated his triumphs on the battlefield. The last had been in 1944 at Amiens in France when he and Oberst Ullrich brought the remnants of the Wehrmacht across the Seine from Normandy in relatively good order. Then they had gotten drunk in a sidewalk café and now Clemens intended to renew the custom.

Humming "Lili Marlene," he pulled off his fatigues and washed in a basin of cold water. As he put on a clean pair of shorts and undershirt, the gunfire from the front grew louder and dirt cascaded down onto his freshly laundered uniform laid out on the bed. Clemens was clucking impatiently and brushing it off when an Egyptian officer burst in shouting: "The Israelis are across the canal."

Clemens rushed out into the darkness to see a line of red and white tracer bullets stitching across the sand toward him. He hesitated, turned to go back inside and get dressed, and then three mortar shells exploded around him and he ran, away from the bunker, to the west, dressed only in his underwear.

The Israeli intelligence officer looked sharply at the commando captain standing before him. "You went across the canal last night on a reconnaissance mission?"

"Correct. We were supposed to gather prisoners and possibly something from a SAM site."

"And you found these things in a deserted bunker?"

"Correct. We left behind one charred steak, a table setting for one, a pair of used fatigues, and combat shoes."

The intelligence man sifted through the material on his desk. "Bonafide West German passport, as far as I can see.'' He was staring at the glossy likeness of the neatly bearded Horst Clemens.

"Clemens. Where do I remember that name from? And what the hell was he doing with the Egyptian army? I thought the last Nazis left in 1964 when we upset their rocket development for Nasser.''

"This guy must be some kind of a fanatic."

"Either that, Captain, or we're dealing with the last of the great romantics.'' He switched on the intercom: "How does it fit?"

In a moment the door opened and an aide walked in, came to a halt before the desk, clicked his heels, and saluted.

"Perfect, mein herr,'' he shouted and they all laughed.

The aide was dressed in the uniform of a Nazi major. On his chest were six rows of ribbons and around his throat was one of the most prized decorations a German soldier could receive for bravery. He was wearing the Knight's Cross.

"That's what we found, I swear to God. Neatly laid out on his cot, mended here and there over the years, and the black boots were right under the bed.''

"Some nut I guess, but somebody thinks he's worthwhile. Two people in fact.''

The intelligence officer waved some letters. "This one from an Oberst Ullrich talks about another job in Germany, starting after October fifteenth. And this one is interesting. Apparently he started it to a girlfriend but never finished.

" 'Liebchen: Though you have not written me here I can understand, knowing your busy schedule. I have good news. Leaving from Alexandria on the fifteenth for home and another project. How about the same meeting place . . .'

"It ends there but he must be doing a good job for somebody. Did you find anything else?"

"No, no other papers. I had the feeling this bunker was a place he just moved into . . ."

"Thanks, Captain, you've made my day a lot more interesting than most."

As the commando left, the intelligence officer told his aide: "Find Laor. This one should be easy for him."

Avram Laor was blond, looking much younger than his forty-five years. He always wore black pinstripe suits, bought in Saville Row in lots of three. He constantly smoked a pipe, one of twenty-seven also purchased in London shops. Laor's hobbies ran to scuba diving, from the Red Sea to Grand Cayman; horse breeding in Ireland, where he owned several hundred acres; and gun collecting, especially shotguns, some of which had cost him over two thousand dollars.

Laor had a passion for guns, which he first learned to use as a young man on the Golan, when Syrian raiders infiltrated every night and forced the inhabitants into firefights. That training followed him into the Shin Bet, where he perfected his knowledge of weapons. For Avram Laor had become an assassin, who tracked down and eliminated Arab terrorists. In eleven years he closed twenty-one dossiers on fedayeen, whom he followed around the world as they plotted attacks upon the Israeli state. In that time he also acquired another specialty. Since his parents had died in Mauthausen concentration camp, he considered all Germans evil and always volunteered when the organization discovered the whereabouts of a Nazi they wanted dead. Three times he undertook such delicate assignments and in each case the victim died of apparently

67

natural causes. And each time newspapers reported it that way so that no adverse reaction eroded Israel's position in the world community.

In the matter of Horst Clemens, Avram Laor was a natural selection as investigator and judge. When he left Tel Aviv, his instructions from the Shin Bet were flexible: "Find the man, check why he was in Egypt, and who sent him there. Then, if he poses a danger, kill him."

On October 15, Laor introduced himself to Clemens's landlady in Bad Homburg as an insurance adjuster trying to settle a claim on his behalf. She had no idea where Clemens was, only that he had gone away at the end of April. When Laor asked about acquaintances she mentioned a weekly luncheon he attended at the Hotel Dreesen. She was also positive that Clemens never entertained anyone, male or female, in his home.

After she went out to shop, Laor picked the lock on Clemens's apartment and let himself in. He rummaged through each room carefully and on a shelf in the closet found a bankbook; some eight thousand deutschemarks hoarded over several years and then suddenly more than twenty-five thousand in one April notation. Laor put the passbook back in place and went out to interview Clemens's friends.

All the men from the Dreesen weekly luncheons were in the city and all spoke freely with the affable insurance man. None knew where Clemens was; in fact no one had even gotten a postcard from him. Laor quickly realized that, except for their roundtable discussions at the Dreesen on Tuesdays, the group did not socialize. When he asked about Clemens's lady friends, they all pleaded ignorance. But one man gave Laor a further contact. He mentioned that during years of war games studies, Clemens referred

frequently to his commanding officer in the war, an Oberst
Ullrich from Stuttgart, whom he practically worshipped.

Laor was in Stuttgart the next day, where he learned that
Ullrich was a seventy-year-old construction company
president. He followed the man from work to home,
familiarizing himself with his routine. When he decided
on a course of action, Laor phoned Ullrich at his office:

"Herr Oberst, I need your help."

"You're an old comrade?" Ullrich sounded wary.

"Yes, sir. From your Pioneer Battalions."

"Which one?"

"The Three hundred fifth. At Voronezh."

"Ah, yes."

"Wasn't Clemens there with you?"

The phone was silent for a moment, then Ullrich
wheezed: "You knew him?"

"I just met him again, Colonel, in Egypt."

Ullrich hung up and Laor waited across the street in the
phone booth. Five minutes later, the flustered old man
charged down the front steps and looked wildly about for a
taxi. When none appeared, he ran up the street toward the
intersection, where a cab suddenly rounded the corner.
Ullrich started shouting at it and then he was out in the path
of a Mercedes which swerved frantically and missed him
by inches. Ullrich staggered back to the curb, his hand
clutching at his chest. Reaching a lamppost, he held onto it
for a brief minute before sliding into the gutter, where he
lay face down.

When Laor reached the front of the gathering crowd, a
doctor had just put away his stethoscope. "It seems to
have been a heart attack."

The funeral was huge, a tribute to one of the city's
leading citizens. The pastor's eulogy referred several

times to Ullrich's exemplary record during the war; his widow wept along with most of the congregation as her husband's casket was lowered into the ground.

Avram Laor went to Ullrich's office that night, opened his private wall safe, and found absolutely nothing to connect Horst Clemens with the deceased. As he rode a train on to Frankfurt the next day, the frustrated Israeli cursed himself for his impatience in trying to smoke out the truth. His chief lead had died on him and he was now stymied in his search for the elusive man from the west bank of the Suez Canal.

12

The news of Oberst Ullrich's death reached Horst Clemens at a laboratory just ten miles outside of Stuttgart. It left him despondent and filled with foreboding about his own future.

He had returned to Germany on October 15, as planned, despite his ludicrous retreat from the Israelis at the Suez Canal. Ullrich had met him at the airport and at a nearby weinstube outlined the next job. When Clemens balked immediately, refusing to be part of such a scheme, Ullrich argued heatedly with him, finally calling on their long friendship to persuade Clemens over to his side. The engineer continued to refuse, and the oberst began to plead. His eyes moistened with tears, his hands shook, and he suddenly looked pitiable.

"Why would you be part of this? I have to know," Clemens asked curtly.

"Look, it's for the good of the country. That's enough, isn't it?"

"No, it isn't. Helping the country is one thing, but this situation is not for you and me. It's one thing to wage war, but . . ." Clemens shook his head.

Ullrich's voice was mournful as he wiped at his face with a handkerchief. "God knows I agree with you, Horst, but it can't be helped now. It's too late . . ." His voice trailed off.

"What do you mean, too late? What are you afraid of?"

Ullrich looked warily around the almost deserted room, then leaned forward.

"The SS. They're running everything."

"What!"

"Keep your voice down. Yes, yes, it's true. They own me, have for many years. Just after the war, when it was tough getting started, they came and offered to set me up in business. I was so anxious to make good I ignored what they stood for and accepted the offer. Now they want payment."

"That's why you sent me to Egypt?"

Ullrich nodded miserably. "And that's why you're here on this job. I couldn't help myself. I'm an old man now and don't have the strength to fight . . ." Ullrich looked pleadingly at his friend. "You understand, don't you?"

Clemens felt a wave of sympathy for the beaten man across from him and then a moment of personal fear.

"And there's nothing either of us can do, right?"

"That's the problem. If you don't go along with them, they'll eliminate you. And the same for me."

Ullrich shook himself as if shedding a great weight.

"But at least this assignment is the last one. They promised that. And your payment this time will be double. After it's over you'll be well fixed."

"You really think they'd kill us?"

"You know them, Horst. You saw them in the war. Don't fool yourself that they've changed."

"Who's in charge?"

"Don't ask any more questions. Just do what you're told and you'll be safe."

After several more drinks, Clemens gave in, mostly because of his loyalty to the shaken Ullrich. In a matter of hours he was at the small lab, where he was briefed one more time on the project, with stress being laid on its importance in the war against Communism. Clemens went to work immediately, plunging into the assignment with his accustomed fervor, if only this time to cover his anxieties and fears.

When, a few days later, an assistant casually passed on the news of Ullrich's death by heart attack, Clemens at first refused to believe it had been that simple. But then he began to rationalize—after all, the oberst had been seventy.

Burying his doubts about Ullrich's death, he returned to his study of a sandstone model of an underground bunker. Five tiers deep, it was an exact replica of an emergency command center built into the west bank of the Rhine to house the West German government in case of a nuclear attack. By now the thorough Clemens had memorized almost every detail of the fortress, even to a set of blueprints providing him with layouts of the air-conditioning system and electrical circuitry.

After a week of intense concentration, he knew the details of the headquarters better than its architects, and was ready for the next step. He ordered fifty pounds of plastique dynamite readied for testing in the morning.

13

Dieter Speck continued to amaze Matt Corcoran. For more than a week since his release from Yelabuga and arrival back in West Germany, the former SS colonel remained the same stolid figure. Nothing seemed to faze him, not the ride on the jetliner, nor the sight of highways clogged with new-model cars. Food and drink appealed to him, however, and over full-course meals, washed down by fine wines, he showed some signs of enthusiasm. It was only when Corcoran drove him into the Swabian hill country, and he walked the land of his family farm, that Speck finally exhibited any great enthusiasm. At first he just stared morosely at his home, now occupied by strangers. But then, wandering the surrounding meadows where his cattle once grazed, the spot where his mother and father held picnics on Sundays, he began to laugh almost boyishly. With relish, he recalled the tree behind which he first kissed a girl, and where he smoked a forbidden cigar filched from a box of his father's favorite brand. The visit seemed to do wonders for Speck's attitude.

On the ride back to Frankfurt, he thanked Corcoran profusely for the opportunity to go home, which the American shrugged off.

"Now let's get it straight. We want two things from you. Identify Radel precisely. Is he really Bleemer? And then, if he is, what he's up to."

"I understand. The identification will be simple. But

beyond that I can't be sure he'll take me into his confidence. Twenty-eight years is so long. A lifetime, even among old friends.''

''Well, we'll have to play that one by ear. If you two were as close as you say, I can't see him turning you away and I can't see him not trusting you.'' Corcoran jammed on the brakes as he drove down the autobahn ramp and entered busy traffic leading toward the main railroad station in Frankfurt.

''Speck, just don't forget our deal. I'm no humanitarian. I want results.''

''Of course.'' Speck snapped his answer like an officer receiving a set of orders. ''I appreciate what you have done for me.''

''Okay. Leave here tomorrow. Make yourself known to this guy's friends. Call me as soon as you get a fix on him. If you can't get a safe place to speak from, send a postcard.''

Corcoran let Speck out in front of the cavernous railroad station and the German walked down the Kaiserstrasse, an avenue jammed with hundreds of American soldiers wandering the sidewalks in search of liquor and women. Speck threaded his way through the jostling crowds, studiously ignoring the shills trying to lure men into girlie shows.

Out in the street, prostitutes had double-parked their Mercedes 280 SLs, and were calling out prices and inducements to prospects. Speck paused to stare at one woman, who after beckoning to him, smiled, and slowly unbuttoned her blouse. Speck stood transfixed, as he leered at her breasts. Then someone beside him was laughing at the scene and Speck turned away quickly and found refuge in a maze of side streets.

Damn women. The last time one of them distracted him

it had cost him most of his life. The Czech girl, Irina. The Russians had been closing on Prague and he and two other Germans had been living in a cellar while they destroyed records of their involvement in the extermination program. It was the brandy that triggered them to drag the girl off the streets and rape her for two days. Tied to a bed, with a rag stuffed in her mouth, she could only stare wildly at Speck while he abused her.

As those awful memories assailed him, Speck arrived at his rooming house and fumbled for the key to his apartment. Because he had dallied too long with Irina, the Russians trapped him in the cellar. While a Soviet officer sifted the incriminating material Speck had neglected to burn, a soldier pulled the rag from Irina's mouth and she screamed over and over. And then the Russian officer realized the enormity of the documents he was reading. He rushed over to Speck and smashed him to the ground. The rest of his men joined in and hit Speck with rifle butts and fists until he began to sink into unconsciousness. But the last thing he heard was that laugh, a cackle rising from the bed. The girl Irina was laughing at him, gloating at his pain. And the memory of that mocking sound stayed with Speck for years, through the interminable days and nights on the barren Russian tundra.

It was his own fault, he told himself for the thousandth time as he entered his dingy apartment and snapped on the light. Because of that one mistake he had condemned himself to the purgatory at Yelabuga.

As he bent to take off his shoes, he cursed the name Irina.

14

The tall man with the hooked nose looked down from the window of his spacious study at the magnificent view. Far below, the waters of Lake Constance had been whipped into a froth by a moaning north wind. On the near shoreline, houses in the town of Lindau hugged the steep banks in a crazy-quilt pattern. To the south the jagged Austrian Alps hovered serenely, beckoning tourists to fresh snowfields blanketing the upper slopes.

The man at the window sighed wistfully as he thought of his passion for skiing and then he sagged back into a leather chair and turned to his desk to edit yet another speech. He had grown tired of the rallies, the constant travel across Germany to establish his legitimacy. In the next fifteen days, he would speak to at least ten groups. But the publicity was important to the cause, the contacts he would nurture were vital to the general plan.

As he scribbled some ideas in the margin of the typed paper, a buzzer sounded on the intercom.

"He's here, sir."

"What do you think?"

"Hard to say. Maybe West German intelligence, or working for the Americans. He's an unusual one, though. Could be harmless."

"What do you mean, unusual?"

"Well, he's dressed in a suit right out of nineteen fifty. Flappy pants like the Russians wear. And he's definitely an old army man judging by the way he responds to questions. Even his posture is pretty erect for someone his age.''

"How old?"

"Fifty-five, sixty."

"Did he say anything special?"

"Just that he wants to see you. Says he knows you. Exactly what he's been talking about down in Lindau."

"Fine. I'll be there shortly."

Ten minutes later, the hook-nosed man stood before a two-way mirror and watched while his bodyguards escorted someone to a chair. In the dim light he remained a shadowy stranger and then someone switched on several lamps and the man behind the mirror sucked in his breath. Abruptly, he moved closer for a better look and examined the square, pockmarked face before fumbling for a microphone.

"Am I supposed to know you?" His voice boomed into the other room.

"I am Dieter Speck."

The man's hand tightened on the microphone.

"I know no Speck. Your home town?"

"Calw in Swabia."

"How do you know me?"

"I was your immediate subordinate from nineteen forty-one to forty-five."

"In what unit?"

"AMT IV B 4; relocation of undesirables."

The man behind the mirror began to pace agitatedly as he talked.

"I was not in the SS. I was a member of the Two hundred ninety-fifth Infantry Division, wounded in Russia and invalided for the rest of the war."

"If you are Karl Radel, that may be true."

"Then who do you think I am?"

"Standartenfuhrer August Bleemer." Speck's voice betrayed a tinge of awe as he proudly said the title.

"What makes you think that?"

"I saw your picture in the paper a month ago."

"Perhaps a case of mistaken identity?"

"Perhaps."

A silence grew between the two men as they fenced with each other through the mirror.

"If you saw my picture in the paper, what took you so long to get here? Why didn't you come earlier?"

"Because I've been in a Russian jail for twenty-eight years."

The hook-nosed man struggled to control himself as he heard this incredible news.

"The last German soldiers came home in nineteen fifty-five."

"No, sir. There are still more than a thousand being tortured."

"So why did they let you go?"

Dieter Speck raised his eyes and stared directly into the mirror.

"To spy on you, sir," he said softly.

"Keep him there," said the hook-nosed man as he broke off the conversation and left the room.

Five minutes later he was back in front of the mirror, while on the other side an aide handed Speck a photograph.

"Identify that," the microphone boomed again.

Speck squinted at the picture of a brick building, then smiled knowingly.

"Breslau, Edenstrasse. I think number sixty-eight."

"Its significance to you?"

"Yes, sir. I went there with you in June, nineteen forty-four, the seventeenth. We met Reichsleiter Bormann, Johannes Richter, Wisliceny, and a few others. At this meeting, the Reichsleiter discussed plans for the post-war period. We made up the agenda for the Maison Rouge conference, we talked about ODESSA . . ."

"What else?"

"The Reichsleiter designated you as his heir should the need arise."

The man behind the mirror searched his mind for something else to ask, then shouted:

"Afterwards, Speck, afterwards, what happened?"

"You and I went to a gasthaus to celebrate your promotion."

"Where did we sit?"

"In a curtained booth. Someone played the violin while we talked."

"Did anything unusual happen during the time we were there?"

Speck looked extremely embarrassed as he stared into the mirror.

"Yes, sir, indeed, sir. I believe you said it was the excitement that did it, but anyway, I had to help you to the men's room where you threw up."

The microphone picked up the heavy breathing of the hook-nosed man as he studied the apparition in the chair.

"You said earlier you came to spy on me?"

"They sent me to spy on you."

"Who?"

"The Americans and the Russians."

"Then why did you come here so openly?"

"Because once I took an oath to the Brotherhood, it was for life. I don't think the enemy really understands that."

In the other room, the microphone fell to the floor as the hook-nosed man, Standartenfuhrer August Bleemer, rushed through the door to embrace his long-lost friend.

From a café pay phone in Lindau, Dieter Speck made his first report to Matt Corcoran.

"Yes, sir, it's Bleemer, no question about that."

"Did he accept you right away?"

Speck chuckled, "Thank God I remembered a little incident in Breslau or I'd be at the bottom of the lake."

"Well, what's he up to?"

"He talks a lot about a political career. I think he wants to run for a seat in the Bundestag someday. In the meantime he's going around speaking to build a base."

"But why now? What took him so long to make the move?"

"He said after Eichmann was hanged, the Brotherhood felt world opinion wouldn't allow more Israeli nonsense like that. So, slowly, men came out of hiding. In England a Nazi doctor sued an author who accused him of crimes at a concentration camp. In South America Klaus Barbie admitted he was the Hangman of Lyon. He even went around trying to sell his memoirs. It's all a pattern designed to refurbish the Brotherhood's image."

"So now Bleemer is running for public office?"

"Yes, but posing as Radel for the time being."

"Okay, okay," Corcoran said impatiently, "who's he got with him there at the lake?"

"About ten aides, bodyguards, I guess. He uses the house as a resting-up place between speeches. Nobody else has come there since I arrived."

"Phone calls?" Corcoran's men had already tried to tap

Bleemer's lines and found he had installed a scrambler system to evade monitoring.

"The usual. Politicians, businessmen, routine."

"Did you catch any names on those calls?"

"No, it's not easy for me to eavesdrop yet. But I'll keep trying. He lets me hang around the house, doing odd jobs for him, but I have to be careful about getting too interested."

"Sure, I know. Anything else?"

"Well, there's one thing that scares Bleemer a lot. He thinks the Shin Bet has been chasing him, trailing his car. Even though it's bulletproofed, inch-thick glass, he gets nervous about being out there with them."

"How close are they getting?"

"Well, at speeches, they're in the audience disguised as photographers. Things like that."

"Okay, I'll check it out. Call me when you're supposed to, sooner if you get something."

"Of course, Mr. Corcoran."

Speck hung up and stopped at the bar for a stein of beer. In the corner a girl in a flowered peasant dress began swaying to a rock song on the jukebox. Speck sipped the beer slowly and watched her swing her hips in ecstasy. As she moved closer to him, his eyes swept her body and then she was laughing as a man joined her. For Speck the laugh turned into a hideous cackle. He slammed some money on the counter and stormed out into the night.

15

At his desk in the American Embassy in Bonn, Matt Corcoran pulled a fifth of bourbon from a drawer and poured a shot. In all his years as an intelligence agent, he had learned to trust one thing. If all the tumblers failed to fall in place for him within a reasonable time, he knew he was overlooking something vital to the case. Corcoran instinctively felt that August Bleemer was not just a Nazi looking for public acceptance. He had to represent something far more elaborate than what Speck talked about.

"Miss Buddington, book me into London tomorrow, will you," he barked into the anteroom as he drained the glass and quickly refilled it.

"For Christ's sake. I don't need that spotlight on me. You know who I am without this cloak-and-dagger crap." Corcoran shielded his eyes from the glare and tried to pick out the faces of his hosts.

The big light switched off and the American saw five dim shapes at the table. "That's better. Jesus, I don't mind playing spy. But you people make a joke out of it."

"I'm really sorry, Mr. Corcoran. I admit we do get carried away about secrecy. Then again our organization is rather unique and we prize our anonymity." The speaker lurked in the shadows across from Corcoran, who had flown to Shin Bet headquarters in Soho to reach an understanding.

"Fair enough. Let's get down to business. I want you to stop surveillance on a mutual acquaintance."

"His name?"

"Karl Radel."

The five figures remained mute.

Corcoran plunged on.

"We've noticed your agents trailing him whenever he appears in public. And I know why."

"Why, Mr. Corcoran?"

"Because you plan to kill him. Because you think he may be August Bleemer."

When none of the Israelis reacted to this remark, Corcoran continued:

"But you don't know yet, do you? That's why you haven't moved on him." Corcoran grinned and blew cigarette smoke straight at the group. "I can help you on this, but before I do you have to guarantee me something."

"What, Mr. Corcoran? What can we do for you?"

"Leave him to me for the next month. Hands off, in plain English. After that he's yours. Agreed?"

The heads inclined toward each other and Corcoran heard snatches of conversation in Hebrew.

"You have our word. Now what is your information?"

"Your instincts about Radel were correct. He is Bleemer."

"The proof? We must have proof." The speaker's voice was suddenly urgent, demanding.

"A man called Dieter Speck."

"We knew of him. Dead in Russia."

"Not so. Alive, in Germany, and working for me. He has already positively identified Radel as Bleemer."

"How?"

"He works for him."

"Could he be lying to you?"

Matt Corcoran smiled again, as he began the story of the Yelabuga concentration camp. The Israelis listened intently as he revealed the macabre details of the punishment center in Russia.

"And as a bonus I'll give you a few names you'll be interested in. Blucher, Heinkel, from the Vilna death camps, Erny, Moltke from Novgorod, Klaussner the sadist at Chelmno. They're all in Yelabuga."

As the Israeli spokesman repeated the names slowly one of his comrades wrote them down on a pad of paper.

"Mr. Corcoran, we are deeply grateful for this information. All these men have been on our minds for years."

"Now that we have a deal," Corcoran interrupted, "I can tell you the Russians will send us a complete list of all prisoners as soon as I'm through with Bleemer. We'll pass it on to you. Is that fair?"

"We're overwhelmed with gratitude, Mr. Corcoran. Is there anything else we can do for you?"

"As a matter of fact there is." Corcoran launched into an explanation of his problems in Germany; the ammunition dump robberies and murders; his initial belief that it was part of a Communist conspiracy and then his change of heart based mostly on Glasov's reactions.

"Do you really trust the Russian?"

"Yes, I do. It's hard to describe but that's the way it is. We all have strange friends in this business."

The Israeli spokesman laughed bitterly. "How true, Mr. Corcoran. Some of our best information comes from very bad human beings."

"Okay, then, what I need from you is any kind of evidence on this Nazi crap. Anything new. I'm hard up."

"On Bleemer, we have been chasing him a bit. Our agents think the riots at his public appearances are very suspicious. All of them are led by quote Red agitators unquote and yet the police rarely beat heads in. And the same people show up again and again to provoke fights in the streets. In Munich, Hamburg, Dortmund, we've been able to identify maybe fifty who lead the demonstrations. None ever get hit on the head and put in the hospital."

Corcoran was writing it all down as the Shin Bet leader went on about Johannes Richter's sudden trip from Paraguay.

"How about the German in Egypt?" one of the other Israelis asked. "Would that be important?"

"We don't know anything about him yet," the speaker shrugged. "I don't think Mr. Corcoran should worry about that one."

"What about him?" Corcoran snapped and continued to write as he listened to the strange tale of Horst Clemens at the Suez Canal.

"We have a man trying to locate him now in Germany but he seems to have disappeared for the moment."

"Send me a copy of your dossier on him, including a photo, and we'll try and help. Anything else?"

"That's it. We'll keep you advised on anything else as it unfolds.

"Good."

Corcoran got up, thanked his hosts, and left the room. Someone immediately switched on a desk lamp, bringing the Shin Bet men into sharp focus: Keren, the wizened ex-Irgun smuggler; Kalei, the urbane London banker; Moscowitz, the sleepy-eyed owner of a South African diamond mine; Abrams, the president of an American insurance empire; and the leader of the group, Hersch Gor, sixty-two years old, but looking forty-five after plastic surgery removed the scars of Gestapo torture.

Gor reread the names Corcoran had given him from

Yelabuga. "He says there are more to come, too. Fantastic find for us."

"Corcoran is a good man," Moscowitz added.

"That's why I gave him thirty days with Bleemer. We can afford it."

"Can we?" At the far end of the table, Mordecai Keren slammed a fist down.

"How many years is it now we've spent looking for Bleemer?"

"Twenty-eight and a half to be precise," Gor sighed.

"And now that we're sure where he is, you give someone else thirty days to play with him? I say we kill him now."

"We cannot. We gave our word."

Keren refused to quit. "May I remind the group that you ignored my advice on Johannes Richter and look what's happened. Instead of getting him when he was in the open, he slipped back into the jungle a month ago. Not only that, two of our agents are dead. Richter didn't fool around with them. Why do we?"

"Because Corcoran asked us for time."

Keren walked over to a filing cabinet and pulled out a bulging manila folder. Spreading it before him, he began to read in a defiant voice:

"Subject first attracted Himmler's attention with work at Castle Hartheim, where he conducted classes for future camp commandants. The main purpose of training there was to instill in these men the fervor needed to perform extermination chores. Bleemer personally instructed Stangl, Hoess, Kramer and others. Victims kept in cellars of Hartheim for months, being tortured by SS personnel, experimented on by doctors. Bleemer oversaw each phase of this project. The men he trained had to witness all aspects of sadism being practiced. Like schoolboys, they went to class on the human body, analyzing best methods of breaking down physical and mental barriers. When they graduated from Hartheim, they became the elite of Nazi concentration camp hierarchy, ideally prepared to carry out Hitler's final solution. Bleemer did not let them go until they had been totally indoctrinated.''

Keren flipped to another section in the folder.

''We move on to nineteen forty-two. August Bleemer is now sort of a roving killer for the Third Reich. From Russia to France he had become an authority on mass extermination, looking over Eichmann's shoulder as he figured out railroad schedules into Auschwitz, traveling with Einsatzgruppen as they murdered Eastern Jews.

''As we know, Heydrich and he had become close friends and Heydrich depended more and more on Bleemer to carry out day-to-day policy. After Heydrich was assassinated and Himmler made his move to get closer to Hitler, Martin Bormann stepped in and made Bleemer his pet. So while Himmler jockeyed around with Bormann, the Reichsleiter was cementing his ties to the SS through Bleemer.''

Keren broke off for a moment to apologize. ''The history lesson is necessary to understand who we're dealing with.'' As he went back to the dossier, his companions shifted about in their hard-backed chairs and Hersch Gor helped himself to a glass of wine from a carafe.

''Bleemer planned the medical experiments at Dachau, Sachsenhausen, and Sobibor. Under his guidance quacks like Rascher and Gebhardt put Russian prisoners through high-altitude tests, literally boiling their bloodstreams with decompression procedures. They also forced men to lie naked in snowdrifts, and gauged their body reactions when women forced them to have intercourse. All of these prisoners died of exposure. In other camps, doctors infected people with rabies to find an antidote, sterilized women with heavy doses of X-rays, and injected patients with gas gangrene to study the effects. In nineteen forty-three, on a visit to Natzweiler, Bleemer stood beside the first van fitted out as a gas chamber and timed the interval between initiation of exhaust fumes and the last breath of the women packed inside. Witnesses at Nuremberg described how unhappy Bleemer was that day because the procedure proved less than economical. Something better had to be devised and that led inevitably to the ovens at Auschwitz. On this level, Bleemer spent two weeks criss-crossing Germany to check industrial plants for the best crematoria design. When bids followed from architects, Auschwitz became the best-run death camp in history.''

Mordecai Keren tossed the folder on the desk and looked mournfully at his friends.

''I demand a vote on August Bleemer.''

Hersch Gor waited for someone to comment. When no one spoke, he said:

''The usual rules apply. I, of course, shall abstain unless there is a tie. Otherwise a simple majority prevails. For the record. Keren?''

''Kill him now.''

''Moscowitz?''

''I agree.''

''Abrams?''

''Kill him.''

''In that case the majority has already decided. But Kalei should be heard from.''

''I have no objection.''

''What about you, Hersch?'' Keren asked belligerently.

Gor nodded his head in agreement. "I can't argue with you, Mordecai. The man should be dealt with. But I worry about Corcoran. Somehow we must make this up to him."

Keren interrupted: "Don't tell him a thing. It's our business, has been for nearly thirty years. He's just a novice."

"I know, I know, but I don't want bad blood between friends. It could hurt us elsewhere when we may need the Americans."

The insurance man, Abrams, offered a solution: "When I go back to the States I'll see Thompson at Langley and explain our problem. He'll handle Corcoran and keep him out of our way."

"Good. Good." Gor tapped a pencil lightly on the green desk blotter before asking the obvious question. "Who should do the Bleemer job for us?"

Keren had the answer immediately: "We have Avram Laor in Germany on Clemens. Pull him off that and onto Bleemer. Give him ten days to do the job. No more. Clean and sure. No mistakes. Agreed?"

When everyone grunted approval, Hersch Gor rose from his chair and stretched. "Thank you, gentlemen. A safe journey home."

16

At a branch office of the Dresdner Bank in Essen, four men marched through the front door just before closing time. Brandishing automatic rifles, they hollered for quiet and motioned all employees and customers to lie down on the floor. Two of the bandits went behind the counter and methodically scooped cash into burlap sacks. The others walked up and down the aisles, keeping watch over the prostrate people. Occasionally they paused to shout ''Long live the Revolution.'' Aside from that they just paced.

The robbery was the third in four days in West Germany. It followed the same pattern as the previous ones. Grimly efficient, the robbers spent just five minutes in each bank, vanished through the front door, and sped off without further trace.

But in the third instance the ending differed. As the bandits walked to their getaway car, one of them seemed to trip and his rifle fell from under his coat to the sidewalk. When several people stopped to look, all four men ran, jumped into their automobile and roared away.

The dropped rifle remained on the sidewalk.

NOVEMBER 12
U.S. ARMY CID HEIDELBERG TO CORCORAN—U.S. EMBASSY RE: BAD NAUHEIM AMMO DUMP ROBBERY— POSITIVELY IDENTIFY AR-15 FROM THAT RAID. FOUND

"Now, Matt, listen to this," the colonel said as he switched on the tape.

"To the Fascist clique in West Germany"—the scratchy voice had a distinct Hessian accent. "The Red Army faction has struck again. Your banks, your corporations, your defense installations, all are prisoners to our demands. Until you realize that your system cannot survive, we will tear the nation apart . . ."

"It goes on and on." The colonel snapped the tape off and went back to the fireplace to warm his hands. "It's just drivel, doesn't mean anything to me."

His legs up on a hassock, Corcoran drank coffee laced with Sambuca. "I don't know what it means to me, either, except that at last I've found one of those rifles and some fingerprints on it."

"Anything on those yet?"

"No, nor on the car. Nobody got the license right, it seems. How about some more help from you guys in G-two on the investigation?"

"No, sir. I just can't pay more men on those ammo dump robberies. As far as we're concerned, those crooks have vanished into thin air. And now with what happened last night, I'll be catching enough hell from Washington that I won't want to hear about AR-fifteens ever again."

Corcoran was sarcastic. "Last night was another high-water mark for army security."

"Very funny, real cute. I'd like to see you figure this one out. Major installation, one million gallons of diesel fuel stashed in above-ground tanks. Someone or some group gets a mortar or two, drops twenty-five quick rounds in on it from maybe half a mile away. Zeroed in, perfect shooting, one tank ignites another, boom, in an hour it's all gone. Who the hell is gonna imagine some nut using artillery on us?"

"Did you tape the phone call after this one?"

"Of course not. For Chrissake, we're standing around watching the place blow up and the phone rings. Some joker with a thick German accent tells us the Baader-Meinhof Communist group is responsible and proud to strike a blow against Fascism. Click. That's it. Who cares? I have to deal with harder facts and we don't have any."

"That's a bitch. I'm sorry," Corcoran said.

"There's something even worse about this one, Matt. Maybe you're not abreast of things with the army, but that million gallons is like a billion these days. Ever since the Arabs nailed the West with this boycott, we've had a hell of a time maintaining readiness in Europe."

"It's that bad already?"

"Listen, bad doesn't tell the story. The Joint Chiefs are going crazy in Washington. The armed forces use nearly a million gallons of oil a day around the world. We get most of our supplies from Genoa through a pipeline and also down the Rhine in barges from Bremerhaven and Holland. The Genoa line is okay so far but since the Arabs have a thing against the Dutch for helping the Israelis, they're putting the clamp on shipments into the Netherlands."

"What can you do about it?"

"Hold our breath and hope the Russians don't decide to make a run for Paris. I'd hate to think of trying to stop them with our gas guzzlers."

Corcoran sipped the coffee thoughtfully. "I can see where my little Nazi caper falls on deaf ears around here. You guys have something real to sweat."

"Yeah," the colonel sucked furiously on a dead pipe, "and all because those goddamned Arabs managed to put one over on the Israelis."

"But the Israelis have them penned up on the east bank of the canal. I heard that two Egyptian armies are trapped there and can't get back home."

"Ah, hah. Once again you miss the point. The fact they got over the canal is what counts. How the hell they figured it out I don't know, but they got over and that gave the Arabs the feeling they could shove the boycott down our throats. Very heady wine for them. They think they can lick the world now."

Matt Corcoran pushed off the couch so fast that he startled the colonel into dropping his pipe. "Where are you going?" he shouted, but Corcoran had bolted through the door and hailed a car at the curb. "The Embassy," he yelled and the army limousine pulled away and sped across Bad Godesberg.

"Get me that file on Clemens, Miss Buddington," Corcoran pushed past his secretary into his office, where he asked the operator to put through a classified call to Langley. As he waited for the connection, Miss Buddington calmly laid a photostat in front of him. He was devouring the contents as Larry Thompson came on from Virginia.

"Why would the best engineer in the German Wehrmacht be working for the Egyptian army today?" Corcoran asked.

"I don't have the foggiest, Matt. How about for money? As a mercenary."

"True, but try this one. He's working for them because some old Nazis wanted to do a favor for Sadat and Assad."

"Okay. But what type of favor?"

"You tell me."

"Hell, I don't know. What are you driving at?"

"Okay. The Arabs have been talking for years about reclaiming their lands in the Sinai. A holy war, right. Only one hitch. They're such bad soldiers they can't put their troops across the ditch. Now the Nazis come in with a guy who, according to the record in front of me, was the most brilliant man in that field, a genius at getting across water. He steps in, does the job, and sure enough the Arabs are standing on the east bank without knowing how the hell they got there."

"So?"

"So what's the payoff for the Nazis?"

"Beats the hell out of me."

"The boycott takes place right after that, correct?"

"Correct."

"The Arabs start doing a number on everyone who stands up to them. The NATO people for instance are beginning to feel the pinch."

"That's true, Matt. I just came back from a staff meeting at the Pentagon and the generals and admirals are dying over it."

"Sure and that paralysis is creeping all through Europe. France is mad at us, Germany's mad, England not happy, we're all fighting like dogs over oil and support for Israel. Very bad scene. Well, if the old Nazis were looking for a payoff from the Arabs they may already have it. If they're up to something big maybe they're moving at just the right time."

"But, Matthew, that's only a theory and a cockeyed one, too. What the hell are they going to do, invade somebody?"

"I don't know. I just don't know," Corcoran was practically talking to himself. "But think about it, will

95

you? Talk to some of the boys in Analysis and call me back.''

''I will, but in the meantime, I'm switching you to Anderson. He has a message he was gonna send by cable but now he wants to speak to you.''

''Matt,'' Anderson's voice was smoothly elegant, trained at Oxford, ''the word has come down for you to stay away from August Bleemer. The Shin Bet wants him dead now.''

''Bullshit. They promised me thirty days.''

''You get nothing. That's an order from the top.''

''How's my wife? Tell her hello for me.''

''I will, Matt. But remember about Bleemer.''

''Yeah, thanks for nothing.''

Corcoran slammed the phone down and sat for a long time brooding about the double-cross from Soho. As a man who prized his own word and expected the same from others, he was outraged at the behavior of the men in the rundown London flat. It finally occurred to Corcoran that he now owed them nothing. Their betrayal had canceled the deal.

17

New instructions reached Avram Laor at his room in the Hotel Dreesen, where he had been holed up for days. Simply because it was a tangible link with the vanished Horst Clemens, the Israeli assassin had been drawn to this once elegant showplace in Bad Homburg. Besides that, the food was excellent, and the stuffed chairs in the lobby were soft, luxurious relics of a past grandeur. It was in these chairs that Laor spent most of his time now, cursing his lack of evidence and fantasizing that Clemens himself would shortly walk past him into the lobby.

Laor had made one trip to Berlin, to an army records center, where he obtained a copy of Clemens's war record. But nothing in it helped. He had even gone to Göttingen, where the ex-major had grown up, but no one there remembered him. His immediate family had died and all neighbors were new there since the war.

The Bleemer operation revived Avram Laor's spirits tremendously. Packing two suits and a brace of pistols, he carried his small bag down to the main desk, where he paid his room rent two weeks in advance and left orders with the clerk to hold all messages until that time.

As he walked across the deep blue carpet toward the glass entrance, a bellboy rushed up to him.

"Sir, I worked late last night and somebody finally came looking for your friend, Mr. Clemens."

He handed a card to Laor, who read the message on it before asking: "Did this person say anything to you?"

"Well, he wondered whether Clemens had been back at all to his weekly luncheons. I told him no."

"And then what happened?"

"He just sort of wandered away. A very sad person, I think."

Laor beamed at the bellboy and pressed twenty marks into his hand.

"That's great. Keep up the good work. I'll be back soon."

The elated Laor slipped on an overcoat, shoved the calling card into a pocket, and whistled all the way to his car.

With explicit orders to deal with Bleemer/Radel within ten days, Laor wasted no time in getting to Lindau. But there he was both surprised and annoyed to find his quarry gone. Casual questioning, however, elicited the information that Lindau's distinguished lawyer and budding politician, Karl Radel, had gone to Switzerland for a few days of skiing before continuing his speechmaking itinerary.

Laor followed Bleemer into the Alpine region of Switzerland, driving higher and higher through mountain passes into the small town of Engleberg, nesting at the base of a glacial peak. Engleberg had not yet been inundated with hordes of tourists, and Laor had no trouble finding a room in a guest house on the main square. After unpacking, he strolled along nearby blocks of residential and business buildings and in a short time, he easily found his prey. Accompanied by three bodyguards, Bleemer was visiting shops along a promenade, buying items at each place, joking with both customers and owners. Laor kept close to him, close enough to hear Bleemer tell a clerk he intended to try the slopes in the morning. At no time did Laor contemplate using the Walther PPK .38 he was carrying in an armpit holster. As usual he intended to kill only when a clear escape road was open to him.

In the morning, Laor was the first customer at the ski shop on the main street. After asking several questions of the owner about proper skis and bindings, Laor rented the equipment and carried it to the funicular at the base of the mountain. He was nervous, for in all his training, in all his travels, he had never once skied, and the prospect of it unsettled him.

By the time the cable car arrived, so had Bleemer and his entourage. Two teenagers, an older couple speaking French, and Laor boarded with the Germans, and the car conductor took their tickets as they climbed slowly up the side of the peak, past the intermediate station, past the advanced station and on to the very summit of the glacier. When the door opened, a biting wind whipped the passengers brutally but they struggled out and began preparations for the descent. As Laor fussed with his unfamiliar bindings, the teenagers went down first, over a little ridge and quickly out of sight. The older couple went next, flying off amid fading laughter. Bleemer and his three guards vanished as quickly and suddenly Laor was alone. Clumsily he mushed over to the rim and looked down. The sight staggered him. The glacier pitched at a terrifying angle, sheer ice, and those who had been with him moments before were now just dots in the snow far below. Laor hesitated, then backed off in panic at the thought of plunging down the hill. As he leaned on his ski poles in dismay, the door of the cable car opened abruptly and the conductor fired one bullet from a silencer-equipped Luger into Avram Laor's brain.

Five minutes later, the car began its downward journey from the mountaintop, and from the terrace of a restaurant a thousand feet below, Dieter Speck anxiously followed it through binoculars. At an elevation of eight thousand feet, the car stopped, the door opened, and a large object fell out. Speck watched it fall, down and down until suddenly it disappeared into a gaping crevasse. The funicular car hovered over it briefly, then picked up speed and continued its passage, past Speck, lower and lower, and then out of sight to the base.

The German picked up a phone on the table. "Are you still there, Mr. Corcoran?"

"Of course, for Chrissake."

"Well, it's done."

"How did you finger him?"

"We took a chance on coming here so we could isolate him. And when the ski store told us this morning they had a customer who knew next to nothing about skiing, we knew we had him. The rest was simple. Only an expert would dare the top slope and the fact that this novice went up with Bleemer was enough proof."

"Okay, Speck, you got your man. Now what the hell are you doing for me?"

"Bleemer's making a big speech Tuesday in Munich. Supposed to be some sort of statement of policy or intentions. Watch for it."

"That's all? Shit, I know that already. It's in the papers. Can't you get anything more out of him?"

"Frankly he doesn't tell me anything. I'm beginning to think I'm just excess baggage around him."

"Keep in touch, Speck. I still need you."

"I will, Mr. Corcoran. And thanks for the tip on the assassin."

"Yeah, I'll be sure to tell that to my conscience."

18

A man in a long black overcoat walked up the narrow flight of steps and rang the doorbell of the large brick house in Kronberg. He had to ring again before he heard any movement. When the door opened he said: "Herr Doctor Alt, how nice to see you again."

Wilhelm Alt's customary smile froze on his face, and he stumbled back in obvious confusion.

"Surprised to see me so soon?"

"Ah, a little," the doctor stammered and then he caught himself and waved his guest on into the living room.

"Another job?" Alt asked as he took the man's coat.

"No, not this time."

"Brandy?"

"No thank you."

Alt's hands fluttered nervously. "Please take the big chair. It's the most comfortable." Alt himself went to the couch and sat awkwardly, waiting while the man lit a cigarette and exhaled gratefully.

"You did an excellent job in Berlin with the Bormann identification."

"Thank you. I was happy to do it."

"I'm sure you were, Herr Doctor," the man grinned. "I'm sure you were. But tonight I have a different matter to discuss with you." He handed a calling card to Alt, who flushed immediately when he read it.

"We found it in the clothing of an Israeli assassin trying to infiltrate our organization."

"I don't understand. I don't even know an Israeli."

"Well, he had it in his wallet and naturally we felt we should get to the bottom of it."

Doctor Alt was bending the card, creasing it badly as he wracked his mind for an explanation.

"The handwriting on the card says: 'Going to the mountains November tenth for a week. Hope you can meet me there.' Meet who, doctor?"

"Just an old friend."

"Where did you leave this card?"

"At the Hotel Dreesen in Bad Homburg. It's a few miles from here. My friend went every week and I wanted to remind him I was going away in case he tried to reach me at home. He's been off somewhere on business and I had no idea when he'd be back."

"The Dreesen. Who did you give the card to?"

"A bellboy, I think, yes, it was late at night and he was the only one in the lobby at that time."

"Who was your friend? You didn't say."

Suddenly fearful both for himself and Horst Clemens, Alt decided to bluff an answer.

"I don't think I have to reveal such things to you. I've worked for you. I'm loyal." Alt's voice reached a high pitch as he reacted indignantly.

"Now, doctor, calm yourself. Nobody's questioning your integrity. We just have to check everything out on this Israeli. For all we know, he may have been planning to kill your friend, too."

"But that's crazy. My friend has nothing to do with the Brotherhood. He . . ." Alt stopped short, unwilling to go on because he might give away too much information. "No, I won't talk about it anymore."

The doctor's lower lip was trembling and the surprised visitor watched it in fascination. After a painful silence he rose wearily and reached over to pat Alt playfully on the shoulder. "I see there's no use in going on like this. So sleep on it and I'll come back tomorrow morning."

Walking to the door, the man hesitated briefly: "You know, doctor, we must have this information. And we'll have it one way or the other, won't we?"

Alt did not respond. He was only dimly aware of the sound of the door slamming and the man's footsteps receding toward the street. His mind was a jumble of questions and memories. Above all he found it impossible to believe that Horst Clemens was involved with the Brotherhood. Just before going to Egypt Clemens had dined with him and told him that Oberst Ullrich had simply offered him special work for good money. And Alt knew from Clemens that Ullrich had never even been a member of the Nazi party, let alone the SS.

Still confused, the doctor began to tidy up the kitchen. Gradually his mind filled with the one thought that he must find a way to protect his friend from the Brotherhood.

At nine the next morning the stranger returned, rang the bell four times without answer, then picked a skeleton key from his pocket and entered the house. Calling Alt's name loudly, he walked through the living room and kitchen. Met only by silence, he tried the first bedroom and found Alt. The doctor was lying fully clothed, hands folded on his chest, his head propped peacefully on a downy pillow. He had obviously been dead for several hours.

From a nightstand, the intruder picked up an empty bottle, read the contents out loud, and angrily threw the container across the room. For a moment he stood still, rubbing his forehead in perplexity. Then he crossed the room, retrieved the bottle, and slipped it into his pocket.

A few minutes later, from a pay phone, he talked above the roar of passing cars.

"Yes, sir, sleeping pills. No note."

At the other end of the line, August Bleemer shouted: "I told you to forget that goddamned calling card. Now you have a dead man to worry about. Look, wasn't he going away? That message he wrote on the card. Well, call his office. Say he left early for vacation. Then wrap him up in the trunk and get him out of there. Make him disappear. By the time anyone finds him, it'll be too late to cause us trouble."

"Yes, sir. I'll take care of it. But shouldn't I check out that bellboy he gave the card to at the Dreesen? It may be important."

"I told you to drop it. If you don't, you'll pay."

The irate Bleemer hung up and turned to a young Brazilian standing at attention in the middle of the room.

"Umberto, forgive the interruption. A little case of overenthusiasm on someone's part. Now tell me, what orders do you have for me from the leader?"

19

It was summer in the Brazilian Mato Grosso and heat had
so putrefied the lush vegetation that a stench hung over the
land. At the hacienda in the clearing near the Paraná river,
Johannes Richter was spared this discomfort for the
moment. He had retreated to a windowless air-
conditioned study where he was immersed in the usual
torrent of reports from informants highly placed in the
West German government.

Intelligence sources continued their running gossip
about Willy Brandt's blackmail problems. The woman in
question still refused to be cowed by threats and, to rein-
force her demands for more money, had placed a copy of a
manuscript about her relations with the Chancellor in a
foreign bank. A standoff had resulted, except that payments continued to go to her from the special fund within
the West German intelligence agency.

Richter knew what the Brotherhood intended to do
about this particular information. He was more concerned
with a report dealing with an upcoming military matter.

COMBINED   GERMAN-AMERICAN   MANEUVERS
SCHEDULED TO BEGIN ON NOVEMBER 18. DUE TO
EMERGENCY OIL SITUATION, AMERICAN UNITS PAR-

TICIPATING CUT BY FIFTY PERCENT. HOWEVER MAIN
BODY AMERICAN LAND-AIR GROUPS WILL BE DEPLOYED
TOWARD CZECH BORDER DURING THAT PERIOD.

                                        BRUNNER

A dazzling flash of light shot across Richter's eyes and
he passed a hand over them in a reflex action. This time
pain accompanied the visual effects of his brain tumor
and, feeling weak, he abruptly left the coolness of the
room and went outside for a walk.

The sound of choral singing from the white stone
church across the compound drew him into its darkened
interior, where he stumbled weakly into a rear seat and
tried to concentrate on the proceedings.

More than a hundred people filled the pews toward the
front. All were men, dressed somberly in black business
suits. Most were in their twenties and thirties; a few had
gray hair. Many had their heads bowed in prayer. All
seemed completely attentive to the Mass being offered on
the altar.

The priest was the same old man Richter had met on the
day he arrived at the hacienda. His close-cropped white
hair framed in the glow from tiers of candles, he was
reading the Gospel in sonorous tones:

"Be you, therefore, imitators of God, as very dear
children and walk in love, as Christ also loved us . . ."

In the back row, Johannes Richter's mind wandered to a
1944 meeting in Dresden.

*"I'm telling you, Bleemer. We have to make sure we
cover our tracks on those Jews. The front in the East
will cave in any day. The Russians are across the*

Vistula, Auschwitz will fall, so will Maidenek and the rest.'' Martin Bormann's face was screwed into a petulant scowl as he shook his finger at his deputy.

"First make certain you increase production. Tell Hoess to work those sonderkommandos and kapos to the limit so that Eichmann's railroad timetables won't be wasted."

Bleemer turned casually to Dieter Speck. *"The daily rate now?"*

"Hoess says six thousand, maybe a little more."

"Get him on the phone when we're finished here and chew him out. Tell him I want a fifty percent increase immediately."

Bleemer said: *"Go on, Herr Reichsleiter,"* and Bormann rushed to his next point.

"Second, the Fuhrer insists that all mental defectives within the Reich be rounded up by September thirtieth. He's been lenient about this so far but now he wants you to stop dragging your feet and settle it."

Bleemer shook his head. *"There's only so much time in a day. I slowed down on that one because of the Jews."*

"Do it. Use Richter here and Speck exclusively on it."

The old priest on the altar was holding up the consecrated Host to the audience. "Behold the Lamb of God, who takest away the sins of the world," he murmured, and with his back again to the congregation he bowed his head and bit into the Wafer.

While Johannes Richter watched intently, the entire group of parishioners rose and filed to the railing to take communion. The old priest served them quickly, smoothly, and they returned to their seats with heads down, chewing the Host solemnly.

"Be quiet, ladies and gentlemen. The inoculations will just take a few minutes and then you can return to your rooms."

The words were mostly unintelligible to the line of twenty patients outside the infirmary door. Mongoloids, syphilitics, congenitally brain-damaged, they had been delivered to the hospital that morning as part of a roundup Richter and Speck had initiated after Bormann's lecture in Dresden. Until better schedules could be worked out, Richter had introduced the idea of regional hospitals, especially equipped to handle these cases.

"All right now, relax," the doctor was saying. "Come with me," he said to the first one, a fifteen-year-old girl, who looked at him vacantly. He gently drew her into a room and behind a curtain where she saw three men standing beside a chair. The girl was trembling now for she had always been afraid of hospitals. But then she sat down quietly and a man was bending over her, reaching for her arm and feeling for the vein. She smiled up at him; her father had always told her that smiles worked miracles. She was still smiling when the dosage of carbolic acid reached her heart and killed her.

Two attendants pulled the corpse from the chair and dragged it fifteen feet through a door and into the back of a waiting truck. When they returned they could hear the doctor calling, "Next, please," in a soothing voice.

The old priest was making the sign of the cross over the congregation. "Go in peace." He walked from the altar into the sacristy. The audience rose, genuflected as they left the benches, and wandered back up the aisle, past Richter's critical gaze and out into the bright sunlight. With the church suddenly quiet, Richter got up and went looking for the priest. The old man had taken off his vestments and was folding them carefully, reverently.

"Herr Reichsleiter," Richter said, "you were magnificent. Not an error that I saw."

Martin Bormann looked up quizzically.

"You think so? I still forget things."

"Only a Catholic detective could spot that and he wouldn't arrest a priest for making simple mistakes in the Mass."

Bormann laughed, a deep-throated growl. The thought of such a scene obviously delighted him.

"How did the rest of them do?"

"I was profoundly touched by their devotion," Richter said in mock awe.

"One more time then and we'll have it all down."

"One more time is all you have. You leave in two days."

"I know. How is Bleemer doing?"

"With the Shin Bet out of his hair, he feels much better. He's stepping up the pace as planned and seems to be in complete command."

"How about Speck?"

"Well, I was leery of him but his connection with that American Corcoran certainly helped us. Still . . ."

"Don't worry about Speck. Bleemer owes him some loyalty. We all do. All that time in a Russian jail. You and I would have been dead. No. Speck's just a harmless husk

109

now. And he and Bleemer are like the thumb and finger on a hand, so stop worrying about him fouling up."

Bormann pulled a camisado shirt down onto his still stocky body. Smoothing his hair back with his hands, he walked past Richter to the door: "Johann, it's time to have a siesta. Don't forget where you're living."

As the men reached the main house, gunfire erupted. Two hundred yards away, some of their handpicked congregation had begun shooting automatic rifles at stationary targets set up in a clearing.

20

Bruno Altmann was built like a fire hydrant, thick-necked, chunky-legged, and bulging out of his glen-plaid suit. He bulled his way onto the commuter train at Stamford, Connecticut. Juggling a container of steaming coffee, Altmann eased into a window seat, where he made himself comfortable and turned to the *New York Times*. Altmann was already sick of reading about the troubles in Washington. He had enough of his own with that town. As president of an oil consulting firm, he had known for years that the world was overdue for an energy crisis, but nothing he told congressional committees seemed to make a difference in attitudes down there. When he told them that one more confrontation in the Middle East could paralyze the Western nations, they had just nodded sagely and left him in a rage.

Altmann fell asleep reading the financial section and woke up as the train screeched to a halt in Grand Central. Out on Lexington Avenue he hailed a cab and rode the ten blocks to his office in a brand-new silver skyscraper. On the elevator, he smiled correctly at several passengers and then he was pushing through the glass doors to the reception room of his own company.

His secretary had three messages for him, plus an itinerary for his upcoming trip to Venezuela. Altmann was brisk with her, as always, and she had never known how to break down his efficient manner.

"Mr. Altmann, a messenger service left this about ten minutes ago. It's marked Personal."

"Fine, fine." He took the package and walked on into his spacious office looking out over the East River. Altmann plumped down at his desk, rearranged his tie, and quickly ripped open the hand-delivered mail.

It was a photostat and stamped across the top was the word *Geheime* (Secret).

Altmann was staring at his own application form for membership in the SS. Dated April 30, 1942, it had been marked "Accepted" on September 3 of that same year, with endorsements from three SS senior officers including Gruppenfuhrer Ohlendorf, his original sponsor.

Altmann jammed the buzzer.

"Who sent this package to me?"

"Triple A Messenger Service."

"That's all you have on it?"

"Yes, sir."

A practical joke perhaps. But who the hell would know about this part of his life? It had all been so innocent, urged on as he was by his former teacher, Otto Ohlendorf.

When the professor first contacted him, Altmann had been properly flattered, for Ohlendorf showered him with praise for his work at Ploesti in increasing oil production and told him the economic section of the SS desperately wanted him. Altmann had heard of Ohlendorf's meteoric rise within that organization and considered himself fortunate to be noticed by such a man. At twenty-five, Altmann was looking for recognition and with this opportunity before him, he thought nothing of filling out an application for Hitler's special corps. He sent it off without a qualm, then joined Army Group A in the Caucasus, where the German army was trying to seize the Russian oilfields. At Maikop, Altmann stood in horror watching the whole town blazing from Soviet "scorched earth" tactics, which denied every barrel of petroleum to the enemy. He and other specialists spent weeks there in a fruitless salvage attempt. Then, in the midst of it, Otto Ohlendorf summoned him back to the city of Taganrog for a celebration. At lunch in the officers' mess, the smiling Gruppenfuhrer congratulated him on his acceptance into the SS and the two men dined sumptuously. Ohlendorf, fleshy around the jaws from good living, was in a gregarious mood. Over cracked crab from the nearby Black Sea, he reminded Altmann of the Fuhrer's all-consuming passion with the subject of oil and how the SS itself had determined to take the lead in research and development on that vital commodity. Altmann's future was assured now, Ohlendorf continued, as the waiter served them a French brandy, 1874 Napoleon. Swirling his snifter, he grinned at his protégé and toasted him on his new career.

"Come along now, Lieutenant, I have to oversee my workers." The Gruppenfuhrer pulled Altmann out of his chair and ushered him out of the crowded elegance of the mess into a waiting limousine. They passed through the city filled with army personnel on furlough and wound up in the outskirts, where Ohlendorf introduced him to his own specialty.

They were standing near a shallow ravine. Lining one edge were black-uniformed guards, rifles and machine guns cradled loosely. Some of them were smoking, a few, Altmann noted, were taking swigs from tiny bottles of liquor. The soldiers were looking down and Ohlendorf went to the edge, surveyed the scene, and shouted: "Commence."

The guards shouldered their weapons and fired volleys in unison.

"Come here, Bruno." Ohlendorf waved him over, and

Altmann looked into the holocaust for the first time. The pit was filled with hundreds of naked people. He saw a kaleidoscope of buttocks, breasts, and genitals entwined in a welter of arms and legs. The mass was still writhing, crawling, it seemed, but it merely shifted agonizingly as the living and dead twitched convulsively. One man's head even rose slightly as if in indignation. Altmann wanted to faint but Ohlendorf was shouting in his ear, "Next batch," and another line of humans marched from the far end of the ravine onto the warm flesh of the stacked bodies and formed neat rows facing their executioners. No one ran, no one cried out. Altmann had tears in his eyes and he was breathing short, agonized drafts of air. He wanted to scream at them to run, to warn them what was about to happen. But they knew, of course, the blood was staining their feet already, and he could see many of them with tears running down their faces as they held hands, mothers with babies, little children, grandfathers talking soothingly to white-haired wives. And Ohlendorf was striding up and down the edge, his gleaming black boots making puffs of dust in the still air.

A guard laughed at something, pointed into the pit, and made a joke about it. Altmann wanted to throttle him. But then came "Commence" and the stink of cordite jammed the lieutenant's nose and his ears pounded with the noise of thousands of bullets whacking into bone and flesh, and the people below him dissolved into a whirlpool of flailing limbs as the bullets knocked them down, bounced them around and finally tore them apart.

Ohlendorf was busy reaching down with a handkerchief. His face contorted with disgust, he carefully wiped something gray off his boots and then straightened up. "Let's go, Bruno." To another officer he asked, "What's the count?"

"This makes five thousand five hundred. But I think the men need a rest."

"No, finish the lot today. We don't want to fall behind."

In the limousine, Altmann wanted to throw up and knew he would, but only when he was alone. Suddenly fearful of Ohlendorf, he said nothing.

"A little queasy?"

"Yes, sir."

"That's normal. Even Himmler was sick when he first saw it. They put some women on a stage for him and shot them. One ran around like a wounded chicken and he began to scream until they shot her again."

Ohlendorf laughed. "But think of it this way. You have your quota of oil barrels. I have mine of Jews."

Altmann nodded miserably. Without asking, he had known they were all Jews out there in the ravine.

"Mr. Altmann, a man on line three. A Mr. Scheurig. He says you met before in Ploesti."

Bruno Altmann tried to identify the voice as he listened but could not.

"I'm sorry about that photostat, but I had to establish my position."

"Do I know you?"

"Not personally but we have your name and number in the files."

"Look it, that was a long time ago and I never . . ."

"The photostat is genuine."

"Are you trying blackmail or something, because if you think . . ."

"I think you'd better make arrangements to take a trip. A month, maybe more, all within your regular type of work. And the fee will be more than you normally get for consulting."

Altmann was silent, groping for a way out.

"Just in case you have doubts about us, another photostat is addressed to the *New York Times*. They're researching a new series on Nazis living openly in this country and I think they've found fifty so far."

Altmann could see his business failed, his reputation shattered, his life with Margaret and the children broken by the innuendos, the smears against them. No matter how he explained it, the fact that he never actually joined the SS after that nightmare in Taganrog, no one would really believe him. Just the fact that he had consorted with Ohlendorf, who was hanged in 1951, would destroy him.

Ironically, Ohlendorf had hated him after he backed out, had called him a Jew-lover and a disgrace to the German people. It wouldn't matter a bit that he had been ostracized for more than a year by his own friends because the SS spread stories about his sympathy for subcultures. His critics would only remember him standing over the pit while the guns went off beside him.

"What do I have to do?"

Several minutes later Altmann's secretary noticed that her boss was finally off the line. Then his voice came through on the intercom.

"Miss Baer, cancel that Venezuela trip. Make some excuse, say a State Department meeting or something. And book me on the Pan Am night flight to Rome. The rest of the schedule will be settled later."

"Yes, sir."

"And get my wife on the phone, will you please."

Miss Baer was flustered. In all her years with him, she had never heard Mr. Altmann say please to anyone.

Altmann left Kennedy airport that night, traveling first class, on a 747. Over Newfoundland, he went into the upstairs lounge to have a cocktail, and an unshaven man took the chair next to him and leaned over to talk.

"Altmann, I'm Scheurig. From this morning. So far you're doing everything right. That's good. Especially for your family."

Altmann was unable to speak. He merely nodded dumbly as Scheurig blew cigar smoke at him. The man's fingernails were dirty, Altmann noted, and then he saw his strong hands, clenching and unclenching, and for the first time Altmann realized he now had a jailer, a goon sent to keep him in line until the job was done.

Immediately on landing, the two men drove into the Apennines northeast of Rome. The land was harsh, lonely for long stretches, and, in the twilight, covered with dark shadows that filled the nervous Altmann with dread.

Just after dark, the road narrowed sharply and Scheurig had to drive carefully. A few miles from the town of Terni, a light glowed. Scheurig slowed the car, and the light blinked four times before going out. His headlights quickly picked up a man dressed in some kind of makeshift military uniform. Signaling Scheurig to stop, he came over to the driver's window.

"You're late," he barked.

"I didn't want to get killed on these rotten roads."

"No matter. Go on up the first side road. He'll be waiting."

When they reached the rendezvous, a tent city pitched in a grove of scrub oak, a giant rushed out to greet them. He seemed nearly seven feet tall as he embraced the diminutive Altmann and roared: "Welcome to the head-quarters of the Fascist Unione."

117

Altmann gagged at the odor of garlic issuing from his host.

"Hello, Rinaldi." Scheurig coldly extended his hand. "Let's get to work."

"Sure, sure, but first a drink. Some vino after the long trip."

While the guerrilla leader showed them into the tent and began pouring three glasses of a red wine, Scheurig nodded to Altmann, who opened his briefcase and took out the worn, doubled-over map he'd been ordered to bring. Laying it carefully on a rickety card table, he smoothed it out and waited for Rinaldi's attention.

"So that's what we're after," the giant said as he handed the wine to his guests and looked over Altmann's shoulder at details on the map.

"That's it," said Scheurig. "Easy for your troops."

Rinaldi bellowed with joy and raised his drink high over his head.

"Paisans, to the Genoa pipeline. May it burn for weeks."

Scheurig drank without comment and sat picking his nails as Bruno Altmann started briefing Rinaldi on the pipeline he had helped build fifteen years before.

21

Dieter Speck not only knew nothing about the Genoa pipeline, he knew almost nothing about anything August Bleemer was doing. Only once since Speck arrived from Russia had the Standartenfuhrer made him feel part of the new Brotherhood family and that was when he had asked him to use the American agent in nullifying the threat from the Shin Bet. That time Speck had performed his job well and fully expected more important assignments to follow. But nothing really changed. Younger confidants still sat with Bleemer in the study overlooking Lake Constance. Other men, strangers to Speck, hatched schemes with Bleemer during long private phone calls. When Speck complained, Bleemer told him his day was coming and that in the meantime, he should relax in his new freedom.

Speck had begun to drink to dull his feeling of worthlessness. At restaurants in Lindau he now spent hours, swilling beer and mixing with people he ordinarily disdained. Speck talked incessantly and when people got up to go home, he insisted on buying drinks to keep them with him. Once in a while Speck got drunk enough to cry and when that happened, his new friends left him there, weeping into his napkin and feeling desperately sorry for himself.

On the evening of November 14, Speck again came down the hill into Lindau. With Bleemer not yet returned from another business meeting, the sullen Speck had decided not to wait for him like an expectant child. At nine, he arrived in his favorite bar, facing the lake, and sat in his accustomed corner booth. Shortly afterward a bleached blond woman joined him.

At eleven the tipsy Speck swallowed another cognac and told her he liked her so much he wanted to go home with her. They walked two blocks, along a twisting side street to a stucco "hintergassen" pension, where she led the way up a narrow staircase to the second floor. The house smelled of age and too many badly cooked meals and Speck had to hold the bannister until his head cleared. Then they were in a tiny room. In the darkness the woman took off her coat and he heard the rustle as she started pulling her dress up over her head.

As Speck groped for her drunkenly, he stumbled against a chair and fell on the bed. Chiding him for being clumsy, the girl reached over him and switched on a naked light bulb just above his head.

Blinded for a second by its glaring intensity, Speck had one brief image of a pink bra, flesh, and white teeth, before the searing lamp burned into his eyes and he heard those dreadful voices from the past.

> "Speck, the details once more."
> "Yes, sir."
> The men circling him had those terrible clubs in their hands as they always did at Yelabuga.
> "Maidenek, please."
> "We transported two hundred thousand people there over a period of three years."
> "Chelmno."
> "I don't know for sure."
> The club hit him just below the left ear, a light tap, but his head and jaw trembled from the impact

120

and his eyes clouded with tears.

*"I was saying I don't know for sure because my
superior handled shipments there."*

*They knew all this, he had told them a hundred
times. But every Wednesday morning at three they
dragged him out of bed and put him under that awful
light whose beam blinded him. And each time they
made him look straight into it. Like a hot poker it
scarred his very brain.*

*"Speck, you're lying." The voice was harsh, it
always was, and the man behind it was coming to the
chair to pull his hair back and force him to stare right
into that malevolent sun hanging over him.*

Screaming "No, no," Speck lashed out with his fists
and hit the woman bending over him. As she fell back in
terror, he lunged off the bed and pursued her around the
room. Speck's mouth was contorted in fear and he had
begun to rave. He cornered the woman and smashed her
across the face. Then she, too, was screaming in a high-
pitched wail but Speck punched her until she sank to the
floor.

Within minutes, police arrived because of neighbors'
complaints. They sent the woman to the hospital and took
Speck to jail. In his cell, he was babbling again; spittle
drooled from his lips.

After the arresting officers had left, the desk sergeant
made a hurried phone call.

"Herr Bleemer, this is Giebeler. We have Speck here
and he's in serious trouble."

"Go on, Giebeler."

"First he tried to kill a girl and now he's saying some
very dangerous things."

"About us?"

121

"About the Brotherhood. About things he knows are going to happen."

"Giebeler, one of my men will be down to post bond for his release."

"I'm not sure that can be done. The charge will be attempted murder."

"Have it marked on the books as something less for the moment. And we'll take care of Speck up here."

"Yes, sir."

"Thank you, Giebeler. Good night."

Sergeant Giebeler went back to the main desk and the official registry. In a laborious scrawl, he wrote, 15 November, 1973, 0030 hours; subject Dieter Speck; charge drunkenness.

Satisfied with his lie, Giebeler closed the book and waited for Speck's rescuer to arrive.

In the darkness, the oceangoing tug maneuvered ponder-
ously by the famous Lorelei rock below Koblenz and
continued south along the Rhine. Lights from villages on
the west bank cast an intermittent glow on the water but
the ship's captain scrupulously avoided entering these
bright spots. At thirty-second intervals, men on the stern
of the tug dropped objects into the stream. After an hour
the splashes ceased and the tug revved its motors and
chugged more quickly upstream, past Mainz and on
toward the first streaks of dawn.

At five-thirty A.M. the night duty officer at the West
German Defense Ministry received an anonymous phone
call that sent him into a frenzy. Frantically, he rang the
hotline to the Chancellor's residence, where a sleepy aide
listened in amazement:

"Somebody just laid a minefield in the Rhine," the
caller was shouting.

"Who the hell is this?"

When the duty officer identified himself, the aide said:
"That's the craziest damn thing I ever heard."

"But what if it's true?"

The aide sucked in his breath at the thought.

"You're right. I'll halt all traffic now."

While the two men spoke, a barge loaded with scrap metal
nosed around the Lorelei and pushed ahead into the strong
current. At five-thirty-seven, it passed over an acoustical

mine, already rising toward the sound of the ship's propeller screws. Twelve seconds later, the bow of the barge lifted slightly from a detonation and, as water cascaded into the hold, the captain tried to steer his ship to the near shore. It was too late. Before he could even radio a distress signal, the barge sank into the main channel of the Rhine and all on board perished.

16 NOVEMBER, 0650 HOURS
NATO COMMAND BRUSSELS
TO ALL STATIONS:
WITHHOLD NEWS OF RHINE CATASTROPHE FROM TV, RADIO, AND NEWSPAPERS PENDING COMPLETE INVESTIGATION.

That morning, curious villagers along the shore were told that a barge had sunk because of a boiler explosion, and that it now blocked southbound traffic. Few people seemed to notice that ships were not moving northward either.

Divers had been going down for hours when Matt Corcoran arrived to discuss the sabotage with intelligence officers. The last one to surface confirmed the grim story.

"We counted at least seventy-five mines down there and for all we know there are another fifty or more. Some are lying on the floor, but a lot are floating free."

"And the barge?" Corcoran asked.

"Shit, that's straddling the channel almost left to right."

"How long to clear the mess up?"

"A month between that and the acoustics. And by the way, all those mines are Commie. They're made in Czechoslovakia."

"Jesus." Corcoran shook his head in bewilderment as

another American made a quick calculation. "That means no more oil for the troops. And we're down to ten days as it is in reserve." Then he shrugged and said:

"Except for what we have coming in from Italy."

18 NOVEMBER 0800 HOURS
U.S. EMBASSY ROME
TO CORCORAN BONN EMBASSY
TERRORISTS LAST NIGHT DESTROYED TWO PUMPING STATIONS GENOA PIPELINE. ALSO ELEVEN MAJOR BREAKS IN LINE BETWEEN PO VALLEY AND BRENNER PASS. FLOW DOWN TO ZERO FOR TWO WEEKS AT LEAST. ONE SABOTEUR BODY FOUND AT TOWN OF MERANO. IDENTIFIED AS AMERICAN BRUNO ALTMANN, APPARENTLY MURDERED BY OWN PEOPLE AND LEFT. WILL ADVISE . . .

At the office of the Joint Chiefs in Washington, a public statement was being rushed into shape for distribution to the media. It would stress that due to the serious oil situation in the Middle East, American military capability was becoming dangerously threatened. When published, the report would cite, among other things, that an eighteen percent cutback in daily air flights had been initiated. It would not, however, reveal that because of the calamitous breakdown of supplies into Europe, both air and ground units within the NATO command had been forced to cut back operations by seventy-five percent. The American presence in the Allied shield against Soviet aggression had nearly vanished.

On the tiny dock edged against the Mato Grosso jungle, Johannes Richter stood with Martin Bormann and listened while the Reichsleiter gave him some last instructions. Then the old comrades embraced and Bormann, dressed as a priest, walked up the gangway and onto the deck of the Paraná river ferryboat.

After a shrill whistle, the ship eased out into the current and Bormann, surrounded by the more than one hundred men with him, waved farewell to the dying man who had served him for so long.

The ride took more than an hour, to another dock where four orange buses had drawn up to transport the group to Rio de Janeiro. There, at the airport, customs officers checked them through speedily.

"Father Obregon," one said to Bormann.

"Yes," the Reichsleiter answered.

"Is this your first trip to the shrine?"

"It is and I'm ashamed to admit it."

"Well, I can imagine the thrill it must be for you, and such a worthy thing you're doing, shepherding all these people."

"This flock is pretty sinful, so it's a selfish thing on my part. I can't save them any other way."

They both laughed, and Bormann walked through into the lounge, where a loudspeaker suddenly blared: "Passengers for Charter Flight one sixty-one please begin boarding at gate twelve."

The Bormann people made an impressive appearance as they lined up and presented their boarding passes to the attendant. Dressed totally in black, they reminded several onlookers of pilgrims to Jerusalem as they went out onto the runway and into the silver jet parked less than a hundred yards away.

Their DC-8 took off at four-thirty P.M. and headed northeast, across the Atlantic toward the European mainland. In the closed-off first-class compartment, Bormann and one of his aides discussed for the first time a discouraging message he had just received. Dieter Speck had become a problem to the Brotherhood.

"Schranz, we can't allow any mistakes now. We'll have to make sure Bleemer understands, though. Can we reach him from here?"

"No, not until we reach France. The special equipment will be installed then. Better than putting it on here, too chancy with inspectors."

"So contact him by regular means when we land, and be explicit."

"Yes, sir."

August Bleemer looked down at the patient and mourned his suffering. Dieter Speck lay strapped into a straight-jacket, which pinned his arms to his chest and caused him to thrash violently against the wall. He moaned constantly, bringing anguish to Bleemer's face.

The Standartenfuhrer had gotten him out of the police station without any trouble, but in the past twenty-four hours Speck had broken loose from his guards and run away through the dense woods surrounding the estate. It took Bleemer's men hours to find him, cowering in the backyard of a neighboring farmer's property. The frightened farmer told Bleemer that Speck had been raving, screaming about being an important man again soon. Subtle questioning indicated that Speck had said nothing more damaging than that, and Bleemer decided that the farmer had not heard a word about the Brotherhood.

Now the broken refugee from Yelabuga lay bound like a steer, cursing Bleemer, yelling orders to nonexistent corporals, moaning softly, whimpering like a child. Bleemer could do nothing for him.

The message he received at ten-thirty A.M. from Marseilles erased all doubt as to his future course of action. He went to his study, found a black kit, and walked back up the stairs to Speck's room. For a long time he stood over his friend, watching the agonized convulsions of the man who had been so loyal to him. Then Bleemer reached into the bag, drew out an empty hypodermic needle with one hand and jabbed it into Speck's left leg.

As his crazed victim stared wildly at him, Bleemer squeezed the needle and a bubble of air entered Dieter Speck's bloodstream. He died while Bleemer gently stroked his head.

23

"Is this the American spy Corcoran?" The voice was muffled by a handkerchief held to the phone.

"This is Corcoran. Who are you?"

"Corcoran, you're being made a fool of."

Corcoran held his temper. "By whom?"

"The right wing in this country. The Fascists."

"Tell me more."

"I'll tell you a lot. More than you deserve." The voice sneered. "For instance. You've been hunting for weeks looking for your precious ammunition and guns. And then you had bank robberies and that oil depot fire to look into. Each time someone calls you up and says the Red Army Faction did it or maybe the Baader-Meinhof group."

Corcoran was waving for his secretary to turn on the taping equipment to record the conversation.

"That's right," he said.

"Well, I guess it's time we helped you out."

"Who's we?"

"We, Mr. Corcoran, are the Red Army Faction that will bring down your rotten system. But in the meantime we can't stand aside and watch Fascists make headway while you turn your eyes away from the truth."

"Okay, I'm listening."

"Go to the old green warehouse by the Neckar river in Heidelberg and you'll find some answers. While you're at it, check up on who owns the warehouse. That'll give you something else to think about."

As the telephone went dead, Corocran told Miss Buddington to get Colonel Burns at G-2 in Heidelberg. Less than an hour later the agitated Burns reported back. "One thousand AR-fifteens, in their crates, the same ones taken from Bad Nauheim."

"Who's the owner?"

"A guy named Ullrich, lived in Stuttgart until recently."

"What do you mean, recently?"

"He's dead."

"Of natural causes?"

"Heart attack, while running across a street to catch a taxi."

"Wait a minute." Corcoran pulled from a desk drawer the Horst Clemens folder mailed to him from the Soho Shin Bet group.

"What's his name again?"

"Ullrich, Siegfried."

"Was he a war hero?"

"One of the biggest."

"Okay, Burns. Way to go."

Corcoran flicked through the Clemens folder carefully, read until he came to the passages describing his war efforts.

Clemens personally designed the explosive charge that obliterated the impregnable fortress at Eben Emael in Belgium, May, 1940. Without his particular skills, the advance of panzer armies into France might have been fatally delayed.

Ullrich, Siegfried
Oberst
Commanding Officer

"That's it. The sonofabitch with the AR-fifteens was in

cahoots with Clemens. And he's working for the SS."

As Corcoran weighed that connection in his mind, he suddenly groaned.

"We've gotta find him, Miss Buddington. For all I know, he's out there now planning to blow up the goddamn Bundestag."

Twenty-five miles south of Matt Corcoran's office in Bonn, near the west bank of the Rhine, Horst Clemens turned off the main highway and drove along a bumpy dirt road. Beside him in the olive-drab staff car of the West German army sat Arno Portmann, a youthful member of the Brotherhood. Portmann was staring anxiously at the vineyard-covered hill looming before them.

"Be calm, Arno," Clemens said softly. "Everything is all right."

"Are you sure?"

Clemens patted the jacket pocket of his brand-new Bundeswehr uniform. "Our identification papers were forged right in the Defense Ministry." He rubbed his chin thoughtfully. "I'm just sorry I had to shave off my beard for this one."

"But the job itself?" Portmann gestured toward the hill. "Can you really pull it off"

"Arno, I've studied that target until I know every foot of the five tiers. Do you realize there are eighty-seven bathrooms, seven cafeterias . . ."

"All right," Portmann snapped and Clemens hastened to pat him on the arm.

"Young man, when we get through with that hill, the West German government will be minus one emergency command center."

They had reached the roadblock, where a guard carefully examined their credentials. "Yes, sir, Colonel

Boje." He saluted Clemens and raised a red and white striped barrier pole to let the car into the restricted area. At the top of the winding road, Clemens parked, went to the trunk, and took out two heavy metal boxes.

Clemens and Portmann walked from the sunlight into the gloomy hole on the slope and came almost immediately to a desk in a brightly lighted spacious corridor.

A lieutenant stood before them, holding out his hand for credentials while he checked the pink badges on their jackets. "We've been expecting you, sir. The Defense Ministry called yesterday.

"And would you open those, please," he said, pointing to the baggage they carried.

The lieutenant found himself staring into containers filled with loops of wire, red, green, blue, all neatly banded together.

"You fellows must be geniuses to keep this telephone stuff straight," he murmured as he ran a hand through the material and then stepped back.

Clemens laughed appreciatively. "That's why it's all different colors. Makes it simple."

The lieutenant waved them on, to an elevator, which took them down two floors to Level C, where they turned down another long corridor until they reached a door for which Clemens had a key.

They had found the signals room, fifty feet by eighty, with an enormous automated switchboard covering an entire wall. It connected the bunker with the rest of the world. Amid the clacking of circuits as calls were made from various levels of the underground headquarters, Portmann set down the boxes and Clemens began to study his target.

He went over the switchboard inch by inch, mumbling

to himself at times as he absorbed what he had studied for so many days from blueprints and models.

"Everything is correct," he said to Portmann, who just paced up and down smoking. "I won't need to make any adjustments."

The two men stayed in the room for more than an hour and when they reappeared at the main desk, the lieutenant saluted them out into the sunlight and their car.

Twenty minutes later, Clemens and Portmann pulled into a garage beside an old white farmhouse. Leaving the boxes in the trunk, they entered the house and went on upstairs, where Portmann picked up binoculars and trained them to the north.

"The five o'clock traffic is coming down the hill. The night shift is due any minute."

Clemens barely acknowledged the information as Portmann continued to stare at the hillside bunker they had just visited.

24

The American Embassy at Bonn had never held so many men from the intelligence field as on November 22. The critical situation caused by the oil stoppage to Allied forces in Germany had brought more than fifty specialists from CIA, DIA, CID, and CIC to try and unravel the mystery of the sudden crisis.

Matt Corcoran had become a focal point for increasing sarcasm as he patiently explained his findings to skeptical colleagues. In the executive dining room, he sat at the head of a table while agents fired questions at him. At briefings he catalogued a growing list of reasons why a neo-Nazi movement was responsible for the incipient disaster. By the end of the day he was exhausted from the grilling, but still confident as to his position. That was true until Miss Buddington handed him another teletype from the Rome Embassy.

PHOTO DROPPED HERE SHOWS SABOTEUR ALTMANN FROM PIPELINE EXPLOSION IN MEETING WITH FORMER SS UNDERLING AND KGB OPERATIVE EAST GERMANY UNTIL EARLY THIS YEAR. NAME KONRAD SCHEURIG. ADVISE . . .

Scheurig. That bastard. Corcoran had pinned three political assassinations on him from 1965 to 1969. When he sent someone into East Germany to deal with him,

Scheurig disappeared overnight and surfaced months later to continue his dirty work. Scheurig . . . one of Glasov's men in the old days, worked in Italy and Yugoslavia. Corcoran could almost see his dossier in front of him. SS lieutenant Crimea, Einsatzgruppe D under Ohlendorf. Helped burn down Oradour-sur-Glane in France in 1944 . . . emerged after the war as captain in People's Army in East Germany, then into KGB as clandestine agent, Glasov's man . . .

"Check this out, will you." Corcoran scribbled a note, shoved it at Miss Buddington, and went down the hall to another meeting, this time with a mix of military and civilians.

The senior general had been waiting for Corcoran and baited him as soon as the rumpled agent slipped into a chair.

"I'm convinced, now, Matt, that your analysis is just plain hogwash."

Corcoran reddened as every official in the room averted his gaze.

"For God sakes," the general fumed, "I fought those Nazis thirty years ago. And now you expect us to swallow this crap about them coming back in force."

"I didn't say that," Corcoran measured his words. "I said they show signs of making a move for power."

"Well, sir, I want to read you a few things that might change your mind in a hurry."

The general put on his reading glasses and picked up a batch of messages.

"Five Russian divisions moving closer to Czech border. Their radio traffic has picked up nearly one hundred percent in two days.

"Let's see. Twenty Antonov transports, the big babies, flew into Hungary last night. Still there.

"And how about this. All Soviet army units in the Ukraine have canceled leaves and gone to yellow alert. Rail usage to the west increased by three times in last week."

Corcoran was doodling as he listened, flower petals growing furiously across the paper.

"So, General. What do you make of it?"

"Well, sir, the Russians don't ordinarily hold maneuvers this late in the year. And certainly never on this scale. Now you put that together with what's been happening here and we see a very interesting pattern unfolding. Our maneuvers have just started and we have managed to send one lousy division toward Bayreuth, one, mind you, because of the oil. And the Germans have sent just one for the same reason. Our air strength is a joke. The Russians could send up a thousand planes, and so could we, but the problem is they could keep flying while ours ran out of gas."

Corcoran looked around the table for reactions. No one said anything.

"Now with all this evidence, Matt, we've still tried to be fair with your own interpretation of the problem. But," and the general leaned forward to emphasize his point, "it seems your assessment hinges in good part on the word and counsel of a man called Glasov. Mikhail Glasov, I believe."

Everyone was staring at Corcoran now as they waited for him to answer.

He deliberately finished an elaborate doodle before speaking.

"I know you people probably think I'm crazy. But I'm one of those old-fashioned guys from the Cold War, I guess, and one of the reasons I'm still alive has to do with just what you're trying to knock. The computers at

Langley can tell us a lot of things. I know that. I use them. But one thing it never has been able to tell me is how to judge human nature, to feel what a man is like inside, whether he's leveling with you, whether he'll die to save you. When I went to see Mike Glasov, I went because he was and is a friend . . .''

"Goddamn it, Matt, he's a Russian, a KGB chief,'' the general exploded.

"He's my friend.''

"He's your mortal enemy when the Kremlin tells him to be, don't forget that.''

"Maybe, but my instincts tell me no on this case and they've always been pretty accurate. As I said before, that's why I'm still alive.''

"Okay, Matt, let's get down to brass tacks. What has he really done for you here?''

"He assured me the Soviets have no plans to kick over Brandt. He also gave me an infiltrator to the man Bleemer.''

"Speck.''

"Dieter Speck.''

"And what has Speck done for you?''

Corcoran drummed his fingers on the polished mahogany table as he tried to frame a decent response.

"He's worked his way inside and keeps in touch.''

"Keeps in touch? About what?'' the general asked sarcastically.

Corcoran was suddenly flustered.

"Did it ever occur to you, Matt, that Speck was a KGB herring thrown to you by Glasov to keep you busy?''

"Yes, it did, but I trust Glasov. I did not trust Speck but felt that no man would take a chance on going back to a Siberian prison no matter how fanatical he had once been.''

137

The general slumped back in resignation. "Let's take a break while I try to make some sense out of this dialogue."

The meeting recessed quickly and Corcoran went back to his office, where Miss Buddington patiently waited for him.

"I have the information."

"Shoot."

"Mikhail Glasov arrived in East Berlin three days ago. He held a meeting with Polchak from Bonn, Sturmer, the man we've been worried about as a double agent, and Kravchenko from Rome."

Corcoran had slumped against the wall. His voice was tired as he asked:

"Kravchenko, too?" Kravchenko could have been running Scheurig on that pipeline.

"Yes."

"Where had Glasov been before Berlin?"

"We spotted him in Warsaw. He had another big meeting there with KGB agents from West Germany, mostly their bomb-throwing contingent."

"That's great. All I need." Corcoran went into the bathroom and wet his face with a towel. "Miss Buddington, I want you to do something right away. Tell the boys in Berlin to stay with Glasov night and day. If he makes a run for West Germany, they are to kidnap him. If he resists, tell them to kill him."

Miss Buddington hesitated briefly.

"Go ahead, do it. I'll take the responsibility with Langley."

Corcoran brushed past the subdued secretary and went down the hall to apologize to the general and his experts.

25

The basilica of Saint Pius X in Lourdes is the second largest church in the world. Only Saint Peter's in Rome seats more people. Opened in 1958 to accommodate the nearly two million annual tourists to the shrine of Bernadette, the cavernous underground house of worship has almost continual services.

On Friday afternoon, November 23, more than two hundred people knelt before a side altar as old Father Obregon said Mass. Besides the pilgrims who had accompanied him from Rio, approximately fifty cripples attended the service. Drawn to the chapel from all over the world they had already bathed in the miraculous spring and now were offering their thanks and entreaties to God. When Obregon finished the service he made the sign of the cross over them in a special blessing. The invalids in turn crossed themselves and then laboriously rose and hobbled out of church to await the miracles they needed for physical salvation.

Behind them Obregon had gone into a confessional where he sat with the purple stole draped around his neck. From the rear pews, men rose and made their way forward. They were not part of the group traveling with Obregon.

"Bless me, father, for I have sinned . . ." the first said upon entering the box.

"Enough."

"Binder, Barcelona."

"Report . . ."

In all, twenty men pulled back the curtains, knelt on the hard wood, and talked to Martin Bormann.

"Gruening, Defense Ministry . . ."

"Von der Heyde, Finance . . ."

"Scheurig . . ."

"Scheurig, my congratulations."

"Thank you, Reichsleiter. The pipeline will not work for weeks. New snows in the Tyrol have slowed repairs."

"The Altmann picture?"

"We passed it to the Americans as scheduled."

"Good. What about Rinaldi and those other Italians?"

"He's back up in the mountains, but the police just raided the house in La Spezia and found the doctor's list of names."

Bormann sighed. "They never change, the Italians. Sloppy, stupid. Will Rinaldi stay out of sight until it's safe?"

"I'm sure."

"Scheurig, be absolutely sure . . ."

The old priest heard "confessions" for more than an hour. When he came out of the box, everyone from his congregation had left, and he walked alone from the cavernous church toward the lowly pension where he was staying.

That night, riot police stood shoulder to shoulder as August Bleemer's small motorcade sped through the streets of Munich. Threats of bombings and arson had been phoned in all day to local radio stations as left-wing groups voiced their indignation at Bleemer's political stance.

140

"His law and order will lead to another Hitler regime," the callers screamed as they promised to run him out of town.

When the hook-nosed lawyer reached the rostrum of the banquet hall he stood smiling gratefully at more than a thousand veterans of the Russian campaign, who cheered him lustily. They were there by invitation only. Seated at long tables, they paid rapt attention as Bleemer spoke.

"It is time," he began in a low voice, "for strong men to question the authority that allows Communism to prosper in our midst."

Applause interrupted him immediately.

"I can see," he said, departing abruptly from his prepared text, "that no one here needs to be convinced of that tonight."

Amid approving laughter, Bleemer went on to speak for forty minutes. When he finished, he walked straight into the crowd, shaking every hand he could, while accepting congratulations and encouragement from all sides.

Then his bodyguards led him to a private upstairs room. Inside was another group of veterans, all officers from World War II, all survivors of the Russian debacle. But these men were different from those in the main banquet hall. Each one held a position in Willy Brandt's government.

"Gentlemen," Bleemer said upon entering.

The men rose to applaud their distinguished guest.

Matt Corcoran was unsure of himself for the first time in years. When his fellow officers in the agency heard how the general had derided him they snickered that Corcoran was losing his stuff. And when Corcoran finally acknowledged that Glasov might well have used him, the corridors at the American Embassy filled with rumors of Corcoran's imminent departure for Langley and demotion.

Corcoran could fight that, he had enough seniority and friends to avoid such a departmental action for some time. But the feeling that he had misjudged both the threat and Glasov nagged him viciously. The fact that Speck had broken contact only seemed to prove the general's thesis that the SS man had been a plant. And now the worst news had arrived from Berlin. Glasov had slipped away from trailing American agents and was on the loose.

Corcoran pulled his car into the parking lot of the Soviet Embassy in Bad Godesberg, just south of Bonn, and hurried past the two goons at the door.

"Polchak, please," he asked the receptionist politely.

Polchak arrived shortly and stared at Corcoran with obvious hatred. He had not forgotten their last encounter.

"Can I help you?"

"I want another favor. Deliver a warning to Glasov."

"Yes."

"Tell him I'm wise to him. Tell him the word is out to kill him."

Polchak stared stonily at Corcoran.

"Do you understand, Polchak?"

"I understand you have come here and delivered a warning to Glasov. That's all."

"You better get it to him right away. They'll hit him the first chance they get."

Polchak sat down. "Corcoran. I don't like you. I never have. I advise you to leave before I call my own security people."

Corcoran laughed bitterly. "Glasov should have killed me in Moscow when he had me. Instead he's hung me out to dry. Tell him that. Tell him the Irishman finally woke up.''

"I'll send the message along to him in Russia."

"No, Polchak, send it to him in West Germany. We're catching up to him in a hurry."

When Corcoran left, Dmitri Polchak walked up the carpeted stairs of the old mansion and knocked softly on a bedroom door. Mikhail Glasov opened it and Polchak repeated Corcoran's words verbatim to the Russian spy.

"Marvelous." Glasov shook his head in admiration. "Never underestimate the Irish, Polchak. They are a formidable race."

Glasov went back into his room where he pushed his lunch away and picked up a transcript of remarks stolen from a NATO meeting in Brussels. The subject under discussion was the minefield just laid in the Rhine river by unknown forces.

At two P.M. that day, Horst Clemens and Arno Portmann arrived back at the restricted area around the hillside bunker.

The same guard was on duty and this time he made only a perfunctory check of the Bundeswehr officers' pink ID badges. They drove up the dirt road to the parking lot and went into the tunnel entrance carrying the metal boxes used the previous day.

The same lieutenant checked them at the main desk and again he ordered the boxes opened and ran his hands through the many loops of wire. The lieutenant passed them into the interior with a snappy salute.

In minutes, Clemens and Portmann had ridden the elevator to Level C and found the communications room. But this time, Portmann smoked in the hallway outside, watching for trespassers, while at the huge relay board Clemens methodically pulled sections of colored wire from the wall and replaced them with exact duplicates from the metal containers.

Thirty-five minutes later, he joined Portmann in the hall and they walked to the elevator in silence.

At the entrance desk upstairs, the lieutenant looked into the boxes, as usual, and noticed that at least half the loops were missing.

"You must have hooked us up to talk to the moon," he chuckled and Clemens nodded in a businesslike manner, returned his salute, and left.

"It went all right?" Portmann asked anxiously once they hit the main road.

"No one will ever discover those wires are any different from the ones there before. The plastique coating on them adheres perfectly and even if they go over the place with sniffer dogs they won't be able to sense the material."

Clemens permitted himself a rare smile. "That fifty pounds of explosives will blow the war room above it to pieces. It's a work of art."

At six P.M. that night a lady draped in mink entered the Soviet Embassy in Bad Godesberg. She was greeted by Mikhail Glasov, dressed in a tuxedo and fortified already by two quick vodkas. Glasov beamed at his guest and kissed her passionately before escorting her into the formal dining room. As servants bustled about them, they sat quietly, staring at each other fondly.

"It's been a year, Kaethe," Glasov said.

"Fourteen months, Mikhail," she gently reminded him.

"To the future." Glasov raised his champagne and reached out to her with his other hand.

In West Berlin, the Red Army Faction was holding a meeting in the cellar of an abandoned building. An argument had started between two members over the content of pamphlets just run off on the group's stolen printing press. While they shouted insults at each other, the door opened and a heavily bearded man pushed into the room. He fired one long burst from an automatic rifle, counted the bodies, then turned and left.

"This is superb," the lady said as she sampled the schnitzel. "The Russians cook it better than we do."

Glasov thanked her for the compliment, while he buttered a hard roll. "So your mother is still holding on."

"And Papa. He's amazing. Seventy-two and not an ache."

"I've read every story I could about you, the stage play, the two movies. According to them, you're sensational."

"You never saw the movies?"

"In Moscow we see old Hopalong Cassidys, that's about all."

They both laughed.

The proceeds from the Hamburg department-store robbery were on the table, more than eighty thousand deutschemarks and the Baader-Meinhof anarchists were drinking to celebrate the victory. None noticed the stranger who appeared at the window of the apartment and tossed in a grenade. The room exploded seconds later.

Before the roaring fire, Mikhail Glasov danced the samba with Kaethe. The Russian's huge body swayed awkwardly as he tried to keep time to the music but he was obviously having a wonderful time as Kaethe smiled up at him and excited him with her delicate perfume.

"More champagne?" he asked.

"Why not. We can sleep it off later."

In the parking lot outside the West German Ministry of Defense in Bonn, two men talked for some minutes, then one passed a manila envelope over and they separated. From a window of the ministry another man watched carefully while each got into his car, and then, as violent explosions ripped the vehicles apart, the onlooker drew the curtain and blotted out the scene.

Glasov was getting drunk. Lying on the sofa, he cradled Kaethe in his arms and rambled on about his childhood in Kiev.

"It was so great before the war, swimming in the Dnieper, waving to the ferryboats filled with vacationers. You might think I'm being sentimental but I can't think of any bad times then with my family. My father was soft, softer than my mother, I'm afraid. He used to sit in the kitchen and play that damn violin for hours . . ."

At eight-ten P.M. Matt Corcoran reached his office after

hurriedly leaving another stormy conference with intelligence agents. Miss Buddington was there as usual, waving the latest fearful news at him.

"They're calling in from all over the country. Berlin, Hamburg, Wiesbaden, look at them. And here's one from the Defense Ministry, too."

She laid down notes jotted down from conversations with excited field men.

"How many dead?"

"We counted thirty-four so far, if you can believe it."

"I believe anything these days, but who the hell is behind this massacre? That's the sixty-four-dollar question."

As the phone kept ringing in his office, and Miss Buddington received updates on the widespread killings, Corcoran tried to piece together a logical answer to the nightmare.

"Miss Buddington," he called, "bring in two glasses and a bottle of bourbon. We've got some thinking to do."

At nine P.M. Dmitri Polchak knocked timidly on the drawing room door. Mikhail Glasov came out, gripping the wall for support.

"Yes, Polchak?"

"You told me to tell you when it was over."

Glasov glanced at his watch. "It should be by now."

"Well, it is. The last one ended at Dortmund at eight-fifteen."

Glasov put his massive arms around the frail Polchak and kissed him loudly on both cheeks. Then he closed the door and went back to his girlfriend.

26

Miss Buddington tried to beg off after one bourbon, but Matt Corcoran ignored her and poured two more drinks.

"Okay now, we're getting places. Like everybody else, Glasov uses a basic modus operandi. Prague, nineteen sixty-eight. For two weeks in July people there kept finding bodies all over the city. Party officials, police, Czech military men, even some civilians who were probably innocent victims. The Dubcek regime was paralyzed at the top as the survivors looked over their shoulders for the next bullet. Then the Kremlin moved in with an ultimatum and Dubcek just sat there while the Russians massed on the border and finally overran the country. It turns out that the whole operation was masterminded by the KGB, in particular my fat friend Glasov."

Miss Buddington slipped her half-full glass under her chair as Corcoran leaned back and closed his eyes. He whistled in admiration at the scope of Glasov's coup. "He must have killed a hundred that time, cleaned out anyone who might interfere with Soviet policy."

"So we have the same thing happening here?" Miss Buddington asked.

"It looks like it."

"Well, the Russians have troops massed on the border again."

"Yeah, but Glasov doesn't have the West German government helpless, the way the Czechs were. He still has more work to do somewhere . . ."

"More assassinations?"

"Maybe. But bigger fish than he got tonight."

"Like Brandt himself?" Miss Buddington asked.

Corcoran thought about that for a moment, wondering whether the Kremlin would dare strike at the heart of the West German state.

He remembered his conversation with Glasov in Moscow, when the Russian assured him that the Soviet Union had no intention of hurting the detente established between Brandt and Brezhnev. . . . But then Speck had been pushed on him to keep track of Bleemer. . . . Later the Genoa pipeline blew up, and the Rhine was blocked with mines. . . . He could trace the fine hand of Scheurig, a man he knew had worked for Glasov, in the Genoa disaster. . . . And Bleemer. . . . No, Bleemer could be just what everyone thought, an old Nazi posturing around in search of a Fourth Reich.

"Do you think they really might go after Brandt?" Miss Buddington repeated.

"Look, I don't know if the Russians would really dare that, but let's cover ourselves. Tell West German Intelligence to keep a sharp eye on his movements for awhile."

"Fine." She sat there waiting for Corcoran to continue.

"Well, go ahead and call them. Time's awasting."

"I know, but Brandt is in good hands through tomorrow."

"Why tomorrow?"

"Because he'll spend all day in the safest place in Germany. He's going to attend that NATO meeting in the underground fortress by the Rhine."

"The what?" As Corcoran gaped at his secretary, the tumblers in his mind all fell into place and the puzzle was complete.

"Miss Buddington!" he roared, wrenching open his

desk drawer. "Listen to this." He read rapidly from the Shin Bet file: "Clemens personally designed the explosive charge that obliterated the impregnable fortress at Eben Emael in Belgium . . ."

Corcoran shook his head in amazement. "Of course! He's the key. The missing link. Clemens is the one human being who could kill half the German government just like that."

With darkness finally covering the hillside bunker, Arno Portmann had nothing to do. For hours now he had sat quietly in the upstairs room of the farmhouse watching Horst Clemens at work. The old engineer was fussing with what looked like a ham radio operator's set, adjusting dials, checking switches. As Portmann stood over him he saw nine amber lights glowing brightly on the face of the console.

"Any problems with the monitors?"

"None so far. The fuses show steady impulse. But even if two fail, the rest will take up the slack."

Clemens's eyes darted back and forth, until he finally satisfied himself that the plastique-coated wiring now inside the mountain was ready for instant firing.

Suddenly exhausted from the day's strain, Clemens rose and stretched his aching muscles.

"I think I'll rest for a while, Arno."

"I'll go down and make some supper. I'm too nervous just to sit."

"Relax, young man. It'll go smoothly, wait and see."

Of course it would. He knew his job well. He had known every professional challenge he'd undertaken during the war, and even at the Suez. Clemens had no doubt that his diligent training for this operation would bear the same fruit the others had. For him it was far more important that this would be his last assignment. After the next forty-eight hours he could return to his former life and be wealthy in the bargain. Ullrich had promised him that. Another man had come to the laboratory to reassure him about his future. Since he had never given the SS any reason to doubt him, had in fact performed brilliantly, he expected them to honor the pact. Ullrich had promised that, too. Despite what he and the oberst had seen of the Schutzstaffel during the war, he also knew that they had a certain honor code, like thieves, and he counted on that to help him survive. Besides, if what he sensed about the near future for Germany was true, the SS might even make him a national hero.

A national hero again. The old fame had been so fleeting, newspaper write-ups, the picture taken with the Fuhrer, then the slide into oblivion when the Russian army swallowed him up at Kerch. Clemens still had nightmares about that march to captivity. He's wanted to die on that trip, but when Red troops kept shooting into the column, he got mad and kept walking past corpses that littered the trail and then disappeared under a fresh blanket of snow.

The early days in prison were even worse. As winter passed and no one fed them, soldiers started eating bodies piling up in the yard. First Clemens rebelled at the thought, then the terrible pain in his stomach drove him to carve a slice off a man's buttocks. The taste of frozen flesh made him gag but he forced it down and then he took another and it was easy after that. By spring Clemens and many others had become sophisticated cannibals, searching for warm cadavers, cutting out the hearts, livers, and other vital organs as their taste buds demanded more satisfying food.

After he came home Clemens never mentioned his

cannibalism to anyone. He also never talked about the interminable days and nights of loneliness, of deprivation and lack of female companionship. He had begun to fantasize about women during captivity. The closest he came to being with one was at the fence in Oranki, when he noticed a Russian girl out picking up wood. He started a halting conversation with her and, when she came closer, he reached through the barbed wire to feel her body. She stepped back, but smiled invitingly and pulled up her skirt. Clemens frantically tried to grab her. Still smiling, she kept just out of his grasp. And then Clemens heard the sound of a heavy footstep behind him. As he whirled around, a guard knocked him unconscious.

The torture of that agonizing moment with the woman drove Clemens to what he had tried to avoid. At night, in the cold barracks, men were crawling from bed to bed, seeking sexual release. Clemens had always rebuffed their overtures, but his needs overcame the revulsion and he finally accepted his first male lover.

By the time he left Russia, Clemens had become a confirmed homosexual. For years afterward he covertly sought men, anyone at first, then gradually becoming more selective, he chose those with intellectual interests more like his own. These relationships were always discreet. But as he grew older, Clemens lost the youthful good looks that had attracted so many young men. So, for some time into his fifties, he frequented cabarets and found partners whom he normally disdained. It was a degrading life, desperate and dangerous, until he met the one person who finally made him feel worthwhile again. Their walks in the woods, the vacations at the lake, the gentleness between them sustained him through otherwise bleak years. Yes, worthwhile again . . .

Portmann intruded on his reverie: "Food in ten minutes." Clemens roused himself and went downstairs.

Portmann was at the stove, cooking vegetables and a steak, and Clemens got a beer and went past him into the living room, where he sprawled on the sofa. A radio was playing softly . . .

At his Embassy desk, Matt Corcoran listened in dismay as his secretary confirmed his fears.

"Tomorrow morning, thirty senior NATO officers are going to be inside that command center. They'll be there to confer with Brandt and his cabinet."

"The whole damn cabinet?"

"Most of it."

"Holy Christ." Corcoran rubbed his temples hard. "This could be the payoff for Glasov."

"And," Miss Buddington went on, "here's all the personnel who had official business at the hill this week."

"You mean who were not normally stationed there?"

"Correct."

He read the list: "Paltzo, Nelli, Portmann, Boje, Julich, Rosenfeld . . ." The names meant nothing to him but he had not really expected them to.

"Clemens is in there somewhere, I'll bet." He was reading again from the German's file folder. It figured. All those years in a Russian jail, where Glasov probably recruited him into the KGB and kept him under wraps for this job. And the other one, at Suez, where the Russians could have loaned him to the Egyptians, both to get in good with them and pick up the bonus of an oil embargo against the West. Sure!

Corcoran had his coat on when Miss Buddington got off

the phone. "Add this one," she said. "Twenty-two members of the Bundestag will also attend that meeting in the morning."

"Oh no they won't. Not until we search that bunker from top to bottom. I'll call you."

Corcoran waved goodbye and hurried out to the Embassy parking lot.

On the sofa in the farmhouse, Horst Clemens picked up the announcer's words almost immediately.

". . . found by a fisherman. The body had been in the water for nearly a week. Fully clothed, it bore no marks of violence. A spokesman for the family called authorities to say that Doctor Alt had been suffering from an incurable illness for some time."

Clemens put his hand to his forehead and bowed his head, while the radio voice droned on. Then he went to the closet for his overcoat.

"Arno, my nerves need a little relaxation. Hold my meal, will you? I'm going down to the village for a while."

Portmann started to say something about going with him, but Clemens brushed by him and out the kitchen door. Portmann heard the Opel backing out and then it was gone and he was alone with the simmering steak.

On the main road, Clemens was listening in shock to the radio.

"The distinguished Doctor Alt had only this year assisted in the identification of the remains of Martin Bormann in Berlin. He rarely gave interviews to the press but at that time he came forward to positively declare there was no doubt that the skeleton he examined could be none other than the infamous heir to Hitler's power."

Clemens began to cry, great wracking sobs that convulsed him. Blinded by tears, he slowed down to twenty-five miles an hour and then pulled over to a roadside rest area, where he put his arms on the wheel and sobbed bitterly.

". . . perform an autopsy tomorrow. However police officials in the town say they can detect no evidence to indicate anything other than death by natural causes."

Clemens blew his nose and tried to control himself.

When the radio station switched from news to classical music, Horst Clemens moved the car back onto the autobahn and resumed his journey. Though still in tears, he could see the road marker ahead reading, "Bad Godesberg 28 kilometers." He suddenly wrenched the wheel to the left, made a wild U-turn on the highway, and sped back the way he had come.

It was less than an hour before midnight, but, in the last-minute rush of activity before the NATO conference, the hillside bunker hummed with noise. Matt Corcoran raced through the brightly lit entrance to the tunnel and confronted the night duty officer with his CIA identification.

"The man at the bottom of the hill phoned that I was coming up."

"I know, Mr. Corcoran. He said you wanted all security people to gather here."

"Right now. We have no time to fool around."

"Sir, they're coming up from lower levels. Five minutes more."

"Okay." Corcoran handed Miss Buddington's list of names to the officer. "In the meantime, get me any information you can on these men. Pictures, home addresses, anything."

"We can have that for you in the morning."

"Start working on it now, damn it."

"Yes, sir. But you can talk to this one right now," he said, pointing to one of the names on the list.

"What do you mean?" Corcoran looked startled.

"He came in ten minutes ago and went down to Level C to finish some work on the telephone wires."

Corcoran was already running down the corridor toward the elevator. Over his shoulder, he hollered: "Close the exits. No one gets out of here until I give the word."

27

At six A.M. Arno Portmann was back at the upstairs window in the old farmhouse, training his binoculars on the entrance to the hillside bunker. Traffic there was already heavy, as both civilian and military vehicles came up to the barrier and drove on into the parking lot.

Portmann counted twenty-one of them before he turned and asked Clemens how he felt.

"Pretty bad. But that's what an old man deserves for staying out until two o'clock."

"Was she worth it?" Portmann blushed at his own remark, for he had never before dared to be casual with a man he so admired.

"I never mix business with pleasure, Arno. Remember that. I simply had a few drinks, then drove around to relax the mind for today. How's it look over there?"

"Busy and getting more so. What about the gadget?" Portmann gestured toward the console.

"All smooth."

Security personnel had fanned out across the vineyard-covered hillside to cover all approaches to the command post for the West German government. Inside the bunker, specialists had combed all five tiers for signs of sabotage and pronounced them all clear at eight-thirty. By this time, the first VIPs had arrived, admirals and generals from

NATO countries. Escorts conducted them inside the yawning tunnel and down to Level B.

At nine-thirty, the first of the civilian guests drove into the restricted zone. Cabinet members of the West German government, politicians from the Bundestag, they left their limousines and moved in twos and threes into the labyrinth.

At nine-forty-five, sirens sounded in the distance and a phalanx of motorcycles swept up the dirt road. In the cloud of dust behind them, a black Mercedes pulled up and the chauffeur jumped out to open the rear door. Chancellor Willy Brandt emerged, smiling and waving to the army honor guard drawn up to greet him. Surrounded by bodyguards he rushed into the gloom of the bunker and disappeared.

At the Bayerischer Hof Hotel in Munich, August Bleemer sat in his room and picked daintily at the eggs in front of him.

"The plane has just arrived," an aide told him. "Pohl called from the airport."

Bleemer touched his lips with a napkin and took a last swallow from a cup a coffee.

"He says he's ready for us anytime."

Bleemer nodded. "We have time. It takes fifty minutes to get there."

"If the traffic doesn't snarl."

At precisely ten A.M. August Bleemer and his entourage left the hotel and got into a fleet of waiting cars, which drove off to Munich airport at moderate speed.

Miss Buddington was at her desk in the American

Embassy at Bonn. She had gotten only three hours of sleep from the hectic night before, and she did not know how she could survive another day at this pace. But there was one more piece of urgent business she had to attend to. Stifling a huge yawn, she put through a call to Dmitri Polchak at the Soviet Embassy in Bad Godesberg.

"Mr. Polchak," she said. "I have a message for Mr. Glasov from my boss, Matt Corcoran."

"Yes," Polchak answered wearily.

She spoke for several minutes.

In morgues across Germany, coroners and detectives discussed the findings on fifty-five dead men slain overnight by unknown killers. Only one common thread linked the deceased. Each one had ties to the Communist world, either as active political foes of the Brandt regime or as suspected agents or double agents working for Soviet satellites. It seemed probable to officials that the vendetta had not yet run its course.

At the window in the farmhouse, Arno Portmann had seen Chancellor Brandt's car go up the hill to the command center. When he told Clemens, the engineer grunted his approval and bent over his console to examine a sudden problem. Two of the amber lights had gone out, signifying a possible malfunction in the fuses buried in the maze of wires at the relay board inside the command post a mile away. While Portmann stared off into the distance, Clemens opened the machine and toyed with the remote-control switches.

"Twenty-five minutes to go," Portmann said.

"I know, Arno. Leave me alone."

On Level B of the underground command post, the war room had become the temporary nerve center for the current NATO maneuvers in middle Europe.

At the electronic wall map, an officer stood with a pointer.

"As you can see, Soviet armor has broken into the Westphalian plain here and to the north has crossed the border at the Lüneburg Heath.

"For a moment neither side has resorted to nuclear strikes but it appears likely that such actions will take place as soon as the enemy reaches this sector." The officer was pointing to the region around Frankfurt. "Beyond that line, we cannot hope to contain them short of the English Channel."

While he continued with his hypothetical discourse on World War III, Willy Brandt, the Chancellor of West Germany, sat listening intently. Surrounding him were most of his cabinet, other politicians, and a sprinkling of military personnel.

"The West German government would have taken refuge by now in this complex, both to maintain contact with other allies and to safeguard a continuity of leadership . . ."

A German officer excused himself and slipped from the briefing, saying he had to make a phone call. Instead, in the hall, he headed toward the bank of elevators.

"In the border complex around Bayreuth, one American division has managed to hold the Soviets for the time being but . . ."

At Brandt's table, two more men got up and left, one looking for a glass of water, the other for the men's room. Outside in the hall, they too took elevators leading to the main exit. In the command room, Chancellor Brandt continued to pay rapt attention to the intelligence officer.

The West German Air Force plane had pulled up in a deserted part of the Munich airport. Fitted out as a flying communications center for the government in case of attack, it was carrying a crew of five and other specialists to man its sophisticated equipment. In the middle of the plane, August Bleemer sat by the window and watched commercial jetliners take off and land. His mind seemed far away from the turmoil around him; members of his staff were at a battery of phones, giving orders, soliciting information. At times some of them shouted or swore, but Bleemer stayed calm, an eye in the storm.

"Two minutes," Portmann called from his window in the farmhouse.

Horst Clemens stared at the amber lights. All shone brightly again and he knew the mechanism would work perfectly.

"Sixty seconds."

Clemens pulled a telephone close to him and picked up the receiver. His face was expressionless.

Portmann was crouching below the sill, his binoculars riveted on the target area.

"Ten seconds," he whispered and Clemens began dialing. Nine. The clicking resounded in the hushed room and one of the amber lights went out as a circuit was broken in the mountain a mile away. Nine again and another circuit ruptured. More nines and then Clemens dialed the same number one final time. As the remaining light blinked off, a quarter-inch-round transmitter imbedded in the hillside switchboard emitted a powerful signal to fuses inside the plastique-coated wiring.

Arno Portmann saw the slopes quiver slightly and then a pillar of flame, bright orange and red, geysered straight up to the sky. It rose and rose, breathtaking in its fury as it churned and twisted. And Portmann was hollering in triumph over the sudden rumble of thunder which rattled the windows and shook the house.

As Horst Clemens mutely surveyed the destruction he had wrought, Portmann raced to an army field transmitter set in a corner and began sending.

"Valkyrie, Valkyrie. Acknowledge."

From the speaker a voice crackled: "Valkyrie. Repeat. Valkyrie. Acknowledged."

Portmann snapped the set off and turned to Clemens.

"That's it . . ." He was staring into a .45 caliber pistol.

"I'm sorry, Arno." Clemens sounded genuinely sad. "But I have my orders, too."

He held both hands on the gun to steady it as he pulled the trigger. Portmann died with a bullet in the heart.

Clemens stepped over the body and went back to the window to look again at his masterpiece. The column of fire had reached up several hundred feet and was drifting slowly to the east. With a perfectionist's eye, Clemens calculated it would dissipate within one hour. As he had planned. Almost absently, he reached for the phone and dialed another number.

"This is Clemens. The code word has gone out."

Then he sat down beside Arno Portmann's body and began to cry.

28

When "Valkyrie, Valkyrie" sounded over the loud-speaker in August Bleemer's plane at Munich, he clapped his hands together and bounded out of his chair.

"Send the orders," he shouted, and at the wall phones and teletypes, his men released long-awaited signals all across Germany.

Bleemer bolted to the rear of the communications section, where long-range radio sets now tapped frequencies used within the NATO defense command. The volume of traffic had increased tenfold within minutes of Horst Clemens's detonation.

"SEND AMBULANCES AND DOCTORS DOWN HERE."

"CAN YOU GET IN TO THEM?"

"THE TUNNEL'S GONE. NO ONE CAME OUT YET. THREE LEVELS HAVE BEEN BURIED."

Bleemer asked: "Who's that talking?"

"A security man on the government hotline to Bonn. He was outside when it happened. They seemed paralyzed . . ."

Several teletypes were banging out other evidence of official indecision.

"HOW CAN WE DELEGATE AUTHORITY WITHOUT KNOWING FOR SURE WHETHER BRANDT'S DEAD?"

"HE'S BURIED TWO HUNDRED FEET DOWN."

"BUT WHAT IF HE'S ALIVE?"

"NO ONE'S ALIVE INSIDE THAT HILL."

25 NOVEMBER 1222 HOURS
U.S. ARMY HEADQUARTERS HEIDELBERG
TO NATO COMMANDER BRUSSELS
SABOTAGE AT SITE CHARLEY HAS PROBABLY KILLED
CHANCELLOR BRANDT, MOST OF CABINET PLUS OTHER
RANKING OFFICIALS AND MILITARY FROM ALLIED COM-
MAND. ALL COMMUNICATIONS TO COMPLEX
DESTROYED. DO NOT RELEASE NEWS UNTIL FURTHER
CONFIRMATION . . .

"Herr Bleemer, the Reichsleiter has opened up his line."

From the DC-8 charter on the airfield at Marseilles, France, Martin Bormann made his first contact. Dressed in a black cassock, he paced the length of a hurriedly fitted out radio room and conversed with his deputy.

"We're ready here," he said.

"The hill went at noon. So far, confusion everywhere but all messages agree that Clemens did the job right."

"Just keep the line open to me so we can keep abreast."

"I will. You should have no trouble following details."

"I hope not."

Ten miles west of Bayreuth, the American division commander was hollering at his G-2.

"What the hell are you telling me? That German armor has surrounded us?"

"Yes, sir. During the night, they slipped to the left and took up positions in this arc." He drew a curve which

164

straddled two main roads behind the American position.

"Well, you tell those Krauts to get back where they belong. How the hell am I going to fight a mock war if they don't play ball with us? They're supposed to be Russian tanks coming from Thuringia."

"I tried to contact them but they've broken communications."

The general slammed his fist on the desk. "Get my car. I'll go and shove their panzers down their throats."

Sunday-afternoon strollers in Bonn heard the sound of marching feet as a battalion of West German troops in full battle gear converged on all government buildings around the Bundestag. A band led the parade and children clutched their parents' hands and laughed excitedly as they watched the soldiers pass by in perfect ranks. By one P.M., the army battalion had ringed the Bundestag itself and occupied all streets leading to it. From now on, no one could get in or out without a pass.

The list carried the names of more than a hundred men and women considered enemies of the state. Over the previous months, it had been distributed to key personnel from Kiel to Passau and now the handpicked members of the Brotherhood moved from their stations within CRIPO, the Criminal Police division of the West German government, to implement Bleemer's plan.

At the apartment house door in Fürth, the maid looked flustered as a detective showed his badge and said: "Herr Viertel, please?"

When Viertel, a Socialist leader, came out, the detective was curt. "I have a warrant for your arrest."

"Arrest? You must be joking. For what?"

"Come with me, please."

As Viertel tried to close the door his accuser shoved a pistol in his ribs and waved him toward the elevator.

The Mercedes had been flagged down by a motorcycle officer, who busily checked the driver's license. Behind him, a CRIPO man slid into the back seat.

"Drive into the city, Bossler."

Bossler, a newspaper columnist critical of the neo-Nazi movement in Bavaria, turned to stare into cold eyes that sent a chill through him. Without protest, he put the car in gear and headed toward Mannheim.

When the engines began to whine, August Bleemer went back to his seat to wait for takeoff. An aide handed him the final rewrite of a speech.

"Nine P.M. tonight. I just talked to Beck at the ministry and he has TV and radio networks cleared already. Told everyone that Chancellor Brandt will have an important speech on detente."

Bleemer was reading the first lines to himself.

"The death of our highest leaders has definitely been traced to a Communist conspiracy. The order for the multiple assassinations came from a meeting of the Soviet Presidium and was carried out by hired thugs. We have their names and are searching for them within the borders of the Federal Republic . . ."

The American staff car was being held up at a roadblock by West German army guards. A major came back from it shaking his head. "They won't let us through, General. One of them said an order was issued right after noon that no vehicles can pass to the west."

The commanding general slumped back in his seat. "They've gone crazy. Absolutely crazy. Did you try to get their top man on the line?"

"He won't talk to us."

"He what?"

"Incommunicado."

"Well, I'll be a sonofabitch."

"General, we're cut off from home base."

"What's happening across the Commie border?" the man at the Air Interceptor center asked.

"Let's see. They have thirty, no thirty-five MIGs up doing loops over Silesia and that region. A few bombers making runs in Czechoslovakia. Nothing important."

"Thank God for that. The word just came down to scatter our aircraft around the fields to prevent big damage in case of saboteurs or surprise attack."

"Another of those alerts?"

"Don't know for sure. But NATO seems perturbed about something."

Bleemer heard this intercept as he gazed out the window at the flat plains just beneath the right wing. The 707 was circling the airport, holding while he waited impatiently for one more message. He flipped the pages of his prepared speech again.

". . . So that the country can continue to function. I have declared a state of martial law for the foreseeable future. From this time on, no gatherings of more than five people will be allowed. A street curfew will be effective from six P.M. each night until six in the morning. Violators will be arrested and if they resist, suffer the consequences.

"All activities of the Bundestag will be suspended until further notice. Elected officials will be properly screened to protect the German people from subversion and corruption. At the appropriate time, new elections will be held to ensure the democratic process in government . . ."

"Here it is, sir." Bleemer read the message quickly, an ultrasecret code from NATO Brussels to the Pentagon:

CONFIRMED NOW BRANDT AND TWENTY-SEVEN OTHERS DEAD IN CATASTROPHE AT SITE CHARLEY. BOMB POSSIBLY DETONATED BY REMOTE-CONTROL DEVICE. INTELLIGENCE SEES SOVIET INVOLVEMENT LIKELY BUT NOT POSITIVE THIS INDICATES MILITARY ACTION FROM THE EAST. HAVE SENT OUT STEP TWO CONDITION TO UNITS AS PRECAUTION BUT REPEAT WILL NOT ACCELERATE UNTIL MORE OBVIOUS ACTIONS BY ENEMY FORCES.

"And this one too, sir." Bleemer's aide could scarcely keep the elation from his voice.

1310 HOURS
JOINT CHIEFS TO NATO BRUSSELS
IMPERATIVE YOU WITHHOLD NEWS OF BRANDT AND OTHERS FOR TIME BEING. WE ARE CHECKING SOVIET MISSILE ACTIVITY TO GET BETTER FIX ON INTENTIONS. IS GERMAN GOVERNMENT FUNCTIONING?

Satisfied at last, August Bleemer snapped out the command: "Head for Bonn," and the 707 wheeled north and began the run to the Rhine valley, an hour away.

The general was in a rage as he talked with higher head-quarters.

"You mean I have to sit here while those lousy Krauts hold me for ransom?"

"Just be patient, General. We're trying to get in touch with the Defense Ministry to see where the wires are crossed. It must be a royal foul-up, that's all."

"Listen, you may think it's a joke but whoever is behind this has a weird sense of humor. They've just captured fifteen of my tanks and won't give them back."

"Hold on for awhile. We don't want to antagonize our friends, do we?"

The general was speechless.

Over central Germany, a CRIPO member of the Brother-hood radioed in with a progress report to Bleemer.

"Ninety-five percent of the suspects have been taken into custody."

"Who's missing?"

"The top one is Helmut Schmidt. He unexpectedly went off for the day with his family."

"Where to?"

"We're checking."

"Well, keep after him. He's Brandt's heir apparent."

"I know. We'll catch him and lock him up."

Over Würzburg, a squadron of German F104 Starfighters suddenly appeared around Bleemer's plane. Forming a protective ring, they escorted the four-motor jet as it headed for the Taunus mountain range and beyond it the Rhine waterway.

Bleemer was walking around the carpeted VIP bedroom, practicing his speech out loud.

". . . To those allies of the West German government I address these thoughts. Though you might question the events of previous hours here, rest assured that we anxiously seek your support. As a bulwark against Communism we intend to stay faithful to our NATO commitments. As men who have seen this nation gradually erode under the influence of the politics of accommodation, we pledge to renew our vigilance against the Bolshevik menace. Surely the members of NATO must appreciate such a position as you desperately try to keep the alliance from withering away because some leaders have been brainwashed into thinking the Cold War has ended . . ."

"How about adding a line like 'Do not interfere with the new situation in Bonn'?" Bleemer asked his speechwriter.

"No need. We always figured the Americans would accept a fait accompli. They'd never risk fighting us. The German army is their front-line defense."

At the Marseilles airport, the Rio congregation had gathered in the lounge to await Bormann's summons from the front cabin of the charter plane. A few of the men continued to play their roles as pilgrims and held prayerbooks or rosary beads in their hands. But for the most part they just sat and talked to each other in low tones, fearful of betraying any secrets to eavesdroppers.

At one-thirty P.M., the congregation was told to begin the boarding procedure.

Outside the Bundestag in Bonn, a bewildered German battalion commander was having his problems. Though it was Sunday, more than a hundred civil servants had been working inside when the troops first appeared. At first, the staff thought the military display was some part of an exercise but when they tried to leave and could not, they rebelled.

Descending on the harassed captain, they demanded their freedom. He played for time.

"It's just temporary. I'm sorry for the inconvenience."

When his irate prisoners continued to badger him, he agreed to make one call in their behalf.

"Can you give me something concrete to tell them?" he begged his commanding officer.

"Put them back in the buildings and lock the doors."

"But sir, isn't that somewhat extreme? After all . . ."

"Captain, if they resist, put them in jail."

The shocked young officer couldn't believe it. "In jail?"

"That is correct. Have any Bundestag members showed up?"

"No sir."

"If they do, lock them up, too."

The 707 flew at ten thousand feet above the Rhine valley, where river traffic remained almost completely stalled. August Bleemer had his hand on the nation's pulse and the patient seemed to be doing well, considering the fact that it had no head.

"Is NATO still quiet?" he asked no one in particular.

"Not a move that we can't account for. They're back to Step Three. The Pentagon just said the Russians show no signs of a serious buildup back in the Motherland."

"How long now?"

"Twenty-five minutes to landing."

At warehouses in Hamburg, Dusseldorf, and Nuremberg, crates of AR-15 automatic rifles had been opened and the contents laid out on the floor. Outside the buildings, truckloads of men disembarked and entered to claim their weapons. With bandoliers of bullets hanging from their bodies they returned to the vehicles and drove off to assigned positions around the cities.

At one such spot, a squad leader tore open an envelope and read his instructions for the day.

AT NINE P.M. TONIGHT THE NEW CHANCELLOR WILL BROADCAST TO THE PEOPLE OF WEST GERMANY. WHILE HE SPEAKS, YOU WILL TAKE POSSESSION OF ALL MAJOR ARTERIES LEADING IN AND OUT OF THE CITY. EACH OF YOUR MEN MUST WEAR A WHITE ARMBAND TO INSURE THAT NO INCIDENTS OCCUR WITH OTHER FRIENDLY FORCES. ANY STREET DEMONSTRATIONS AGAINST THE BROTHERHOOD WILL BE PUT DOWN IMMEDIATELY BY MAXIMUM USE OF FORCE.

At Marseilles, the congregation had filed into the tourist section, where Schranz, Bormann's chief deputy, went among them to describe the latest reports out of Germany. The tall, blond giant, in his early forties, was effusive as he read some of the notes taken from radio dispatches.

"We'll leave within the hour," he promised and went back to the front cabin where the Reichsleiter had put on horn-rimmed glasses to study another almost hysterical cable:

1355 HOURS
AMERICAN EMBASSY BONN
TO PRESIDENT OF THE UNITED STATES

EYES ONLY

GERMAN LEADERSHIP GONE. BELIEVE LINKED TO
SOVIET ACTION. KGB CHIEF HERE IN WEST IN PAST DAYS
AFTER WARSAW MEETINGS WITH ASSASSINATION
EXPERTS. CANNOT LAY BLAME TO ANY OTHER SOURCE.
QUESTION AT PRESENT IS URGENT FOR YOU. DOES
SOVIET MOVE PRESUME SIMILAR TACTICS AGAINST
WASHINGTON, LONDON, PARIS, ETC.? WE CANNOT HELP
BUT WARN OF THIS LIKELIHOOD AND URGE EXTREME
CAUTION YOUR PERSON.

Bormann twirled his glasses thoughtfully. "Do you
realize, Schranz, if we had the decoding equipment
Bleemer has in his plane, we might never have lost the
other war. I'm literally standing over everyone's shoulder
as they read it themselves. Within seconds."As he pon-
dered the impact of modern technology, Bormann went
back to his seat with a bemused expression on his face.

The seminar had been going on for two days in the lake
district south of Berlin. Industrialists from seven major
German corporations had come to hear speakers on the
economy and relax a little from the heavy workload they
all endured.

At lunch tables set up by the shoreline, the executives
drank steins of beer while one man rapped a glass for
attention. He seemed flushed with excitement and began
speaking even before the noise abated.

"I have great news for all of us. I just learned from the
highest authority that our organization has finally taken
the ultimate step. Brandt is dead and Bleemer is assuming
power."

Someone at a table leaped up and shouted. "Sieg Heil" and the corporate executives followed him as a body and flashed their right arms high in the Nazi salute.

Over Koblenz, Bleemer went out to the radio section.

"How long till touchdown?"

"Fifteen minutes."

"Has the airfield reported in?"

"Dingler says the army is patrolling the route from the city. The reception committee is already in place at the flight line."

"And the Bundestag?"

"No one in or out. Totally isolated."

Bleemer picked up a microphone and spoke to Bormann in Marseilles.

"All checkpoints are secure."

"We lost your last transmission due to static."

"What one was that?" Bleemer prompted the operator.

"The one about NATO."

"Here it is again." Reichsleiter Bleemer read the secret cable slowly.

1401 HOURS

NATO BRUSSELS

TO ALL COMMANDS

BRANDT'S DEATH CONFIRMED. ALSO MOST OF CABINET
KILLED. DENY REPEAT DENY ANY QUERIES FROM MEDIA
ABOUT STORY UNTIL PERMISSION FORWARDED YOU.

"That's good," Bormann growled from France. "Have our own friends in TV and radio been co-operating?"

"Not one station has commented adversely so far. The blanket is tight. Touchdown in five minutes."

"Congratulations."

Down below, the airport looked deserted except for two military transports parked by a hangar. The Starfighter escort had begun to peel off and Bleemer saw one pilot give the thumbs-up just before he pulled off to the right side. Bleemer's pilot extended the flaps and, as the wheels went down on the big jet, Bleemer strapped himself in and breathed deeply, trying to relieve the strain of the momentous day.

"Touchdown," the cry ran through the plane and on to France, where Bormann crouched over the set and strained to hear every word.

Bleemer saw rows of people drawn up at the side of the runway and behind them tank turrets and then some choppers lifting in and out of the terminal area. As the plane turned in a big arc and pulled into its assigned space, the engines cut immediately and Bleemer combed his thinning hair nervously.

Several aides went out first and then Bleemer was on the ground and walking toward Burgdorf and Fritsch, and the others, all standing stiffly at attention.

He suddenly felt a tremendous sense of accomplishment as he came close to these old comrades from the Brotherhood. His hand shot out and he waited for someone to break the spell and greet him.

From the rear of the group, a voice called out in bad German: "Hold it right there, Standartenfuhrer." Matt Corcoran rounded the corner to face his astonished adversary.

The voice on the radio screamed through the front compartment of the chartered DC-8 in Marseilles.

"Something's gone wrong out there, Bleemer's in handcuffs. Go back . . ."

As it broke off, Martin Bormann leaped up. "Find out what that was all about."

The radio operator shook his head. "They've broken off in midsentence. I can't raise them anymore."

Bormann quickly moved to the open door. "Give the pilot the alternate plan, Schranz. And you know what to do here." He gestured toward his compartment. "Then you follow me. I'll be waiting at the car."

Along the highway from the airport to Cologne, the buttoned-up U.S. army jeeps formed a long line. Matt Corcoran sat in one beside the still-haughty August Bleemer, who had refused to speak since being arrested. Corcoran stared in fascination at the hook-nosed man beside him and every so often attempted to open a dialogue. Bleemer ignored him.

As the convoy reached the Rhine river bridge across from Cologne Cathedral, Corcoran tried his companion once again.

"What did you do with Speck?"

Bleemer sat still for a moment, then turned a malevolent gaze on the American.

"I know no Speck," he hissed and lapsed into silence.

Outside the Marseilles terminal, Bormann's aide, Schranz, joined the Reichsleiter at the side of a black Citroen. As they got into it, the plane carrying their charter group lumbered down the runway and climbed laboriously into a cloudless sky.

In the tourist section, passengers began lighting up as soon as the No Smoking sign faded. A mood of excitement gripped them as they speculated on the coming hours and days inside a newly born Fourth Reich. No one seemed to notice that the jet had turned out over the ocean on a southerly course for Africa.

Eleven minutes after takeoff the pilot reached his cruising altitude and prepared to make a heading correction. At that moment the bomb in the briefcase under Bormann's seat ignited and the aircraft disintegrated over the Mediterranean. Pieces of fuselage, bodies, luggage, and seats rained down upon the choppy waters and slowly sank into forty fathoms.

The black Citroen had made a hasty getaway from Marseilles and was passing quickly through the coastal villages of southern France. Schranz looked stricken as he checked his watch.

"The time has come and gone, Reichsleiter," he sighed.

Bormann's voice was harsh. "It was necessary. If Bleemer or any of those people talk, we'll be traced back to Lourdes and the plane from Marseilles. And now the authorities will assume we died in the explosion. No, Schranz, it's better this way."

Schranz was forced to agree.

29

"Keep feeding it to them, Miss Buddington."

"Yes, sir," she answered and smiled beatifically at her boss.

Three thousand miles away, in the basement of Building C at Langley, Virginia, a group of CIA officers read the uncoded breakout as it poured from the computer.

". . . I found Clemens in the switchboard room, bawling his eyes out as he prepared to disarm the explosives. He chose this course of action because he mistrusted West German intelligence, in case the SS had men there. And he had a feeling the Americans might laugh him out of town if he suddenly blurted out his wild story to them. Of course, here Clemens must have had a sixth sense . . ."

"Corcoran's really breaking it off in us, isn't he?" Larry Thompson grinned in appreciation.

". . . Once he filled us in on what he knew—and with what I knew—we could organize for the following day. First we disarmed the explosives to avoid an accident, then sent Brandt and the others inside to smoke out Bleemer's men. When three took off a few minutes before detonation we arrested them outside. Then we evacuated the bunker, armed the weapon again, and let Clemens blow the hill. It was going to be demolished anyway.

"After his partner sent the code word, we just waited for whoever came out of the woodwork. We sent a few phony cables, messages to suck Bleemer along while we followed his flight in. Then we picked off the other ringleaders as they stood around with their hands in the cookie jar. Quite simple for an experienced field man like me.''

''That Irishman will never let go the jugular after this one,'' Thompson murmured.

''Aren't you gonna remind him,'' someone asked Thompson, ''that it was Clemens who really saved his bacon?''

''Yeah,'' Thompson agreed. ''Evidently Clemens cried for hours when he heard the news about Alt's body being fished out of the water.'' He laughed. ''They'd been calling each other 'Liebchen' for years.''

The machine was chattering again.

''. . . Tell Tessa her boy did it against all odds. And tell her I love her . . .''

''Pain in the ass.'' Thompson ripped off the coup report and took it into the Director's office.

At an American air base close to the East German border, the rain slanted into the faces of more than a hundred military policemen. Black Maria vans drove past them and sent sheets of spray into the air.

The ten-vehicle convoy came to a halt outside a row of barracks and while drivers kept the motors running, several American and West German officers jumped out with manifests in their hands.

Inside Processing Center EUCOM, they sat down with army clerks and began checking off a list of names.

Mikhail Glasov watched the orderly procedure for a moment, then exhaled gratefully from a Marlboro Matt Corcoran had given him.

''Next time I hear you've put a price on my head, I'll have to think twice about our relationship,'' he said sadly.

''The next time you run a goddamn purge in my backyard while I'm trying to keep my head above water, I'll personally shoot you in the ass."

"Sorry about the timing. Same with our Red Army maneuvers in Poland. Bad timing on our part, no question. But orders are orders. My superiors finally got tired of the East Germans calling the shots in the field. So I was sent to pay my respects to the rank and file. Remember, I told you once we didn't want Brandt to have any more trouble?"

"Yeah, well I see you didn't get them all. That agent, Guillaume, is sitting in his office right now."

"I know that. He's the one person I really wanted to take care of. But again we had to compromise a little. Guillaume has powerful support in East Germany and they manage to protect him. This time anyway."

"He'll help bring Brandt down, Mike. You'll regret it someday."

"Maybe. How about one of those Jack Daniels before I go?"

The two men clinked glasses and swallowed their shots. Corcoran refilled immediately, as the door opened and a general barked: "How's it going, Anderson?"

One of the officers at the desk said: "Five minutes tops."

"Okay. Let's shake it."

The general disappeared into the downpour while Corcoran and Glasov leaned against a wall and sipped the bourbon. Glasov waved at the Black Marias.

"By the way, don't ever tell me about your American democracy in action," Glasov grinned at Corcoran.

"Yeah, just like your purge trials in the thirties. Don't throw that stuff at me."

"But at least we had trials. Not like this."

"Look, we all agreed on the best solution. Nobody has to know what happened. At least publicly. But if anyone tries to sniff it out, we'll say that when Radel was about to be exposed as Bleemer, a Nazi mass-murderer, he committed suicide. The same goes for the other top guys. They all died in an airplane explosion over the Mediterranean. There was one, you know—the same day as the coup attempt here. Some pilgrims to Lourdes."

As Glasov nodded, the general burst in the door. "Let's move out."

The officers inside gathered their papers and joined him at the vans.

Corcoran and Glasov hunched to meet the rain and left the processing barracks.

"Take care of Clemens," Glasov warned. "He is really a gentle man."

"I will. I owe him that. He's not like them." Corcoran was pointing at the line of prisoners arranged in a column beside the convoy. Shackled hand and foot, they began to shuffle across the tarmac to an enormous jet, floodlighted and ringed by guards.

"One hundred twenty-four Nazis, every one of them another Dieter Speck. God, are they arrogant."

"But they talked."

"Oh, how they talked. They named two hundred more, little guys compared to them, but out of the same mold. We're picking them up and stashing them for another shipment. Nice and clean that way."

The prisoners moved past the agents in painful strides as the chains hobbled their gait. Hatless, coatless, they were already drenched by the time they reached the plane ramp and awkwardly climbed the stairs.

"And how about him?" Glasov asked.

Corcoran looked directly into August Bleemer's pinched face, as the hook-nosed man ignored him and walked by with as erect a carriage as he could manage.

"After a day with the boys, he spilled his guts. 'Three years in the planning,' he said, minute details of the coup that only a German would love to dredge up. But we broke him."

The last of the column filed into the aircraft and its engines began to turn over.

Glasov clapped Matt Corcoran on the shoulder, then embraced him affectionately. "We'll be in touch."

"Give them the works at Yelabuga." Corcoran broke away self-consciously.

Glasov nodded. "The works. We promise. Especially Bleemer."

They had reached the ramp, when Corcoran impulsively returned Glasov's embrace. "Thanks for taking these guys off our hands. You've redeemed yourself with me—for the time being, anyhow."

Glasov smiled tolerantly at his friend and waved his arm toward the windows of the IL-62 where the German prisoners stared out for the last time at their homeland. "Take a look, Matt. All those Fascists are in there due to you. You got the whole crew. Every last one of them . . ."

Four hundred and twenty miles to the southwest, a sleepy policeman at the Spanish border came out of his hut to see a black Citroen idling in front of the barrier. The driver was waving passports for inspection and the Spaniard riffled through them before leaning in the window to check the photos against the passengers. When he saw the priest in the right-hand seat, he smiled amiably and the priest nodded in return. The policeman quickly straightened up, removed the barrier, and the Citroen sped past him, out onto the road leading down to San Sebastian. Inside, the priest stared grimly into the darkness ahead and wondered what could possibly have gone wrong in Germany.

MORE GREAT READING FROM BERKLEY

OTHER GIANS FROM BERKLEY